MW01537364

SNOWED IN AT THE COTTAGE

A SNOWED IN FOR CHRISTMAS CLEAN ROMANCE

CATELYN MEADOWS

1

———

The mountainside was blanketed with snow. The white contrast made the evergreen trees ever-greener, the sky a radiant blue, and the snow blinding. Grace Eastland hugged her coat tighter around herself to ward off the colder-than-popsicles weather. The last time she'd been this cold had been during her brief stint in the freezer section at Costco. People actually lived with this arctic temperature all the time?

Then again, the winding road, the hush of the trees, and the snow's untouched beauty as it spread beneath an untarnished sky was nothing short of beautiful. She almost didn't notice the winter air nipping her cheeks.

The heavy sound of a trunk slamming closed jarred her. Her Uber driver held her lime green suitcase toward her. "Here you go," he said.

Grace pulled her gaze away from the snowy canvas surrounding her and thanked him before returning her glance where it was. She peered past the parking lot filled with a few cars to the inn where she would be spending Christmas.

Harper's Inn looked more like a quaint home than a hotel,

with dual points on its rooftops, connected by a covered porch in the center. Multiple windows kept the white inn from blending in with the snowy landscape around it. Trees spoked along the mountainside, offering a cape of branches trailing behind the inn. Grace wondered if this scene was what gave the town of West Hills, Montana—several miles out—its name.

Grace breathed in the crisp, open air and the scent of snow. She tried to find a way to describe the smell, but it was the kind of scent that nothing else could quite replace. It was cleansing in her lungs, rejuvenating and filling her with energy she hadn't felt in so long. Stress slipped from her ribs and down to her fingertips.

She needed this. She so needed this.

Jackson Hole had been her mother's suggestion for writing research, but Grace didn't want to be in a tourist trap. Yellowstone was another option, though only accessible by snowmobiles during the winter. During her research, however, she came across a different little gem. Located at the northernmost part of the state, just below the Canadian border, was a little town overflowing with charm. West Hills—and more specifically, Harper's Inn—claimed to be America's North Pole. The perfect destination for a Christmas writing retreat. No interruptions. Just seclusion to inspire her to create the perfect environment for her story.

After her most recent rejection from yet another agent, Grace wasn't sure she could take any more. She'd poured her heart and soul into that book. She'd edited, cut words, added more and tweaked it so much that if her manuscript had been made of fabric, it would have had more stitch lines and random scraps than a patchwork quilt. Even still, she was proud of that book. How could they turn her down?

Grace had been so distraught. One or two rejections had been hard enough, but she'd sent her book to over a hundred agents. And every. Single. One of them. Said no. It was hard not to take that personally or see it as a reflection of herself.

Talking things over with her parents had helped. Mom suggested Grace start a new story. "Rejection is just an opportunity to try something else," she'd said, and then asked what would help Grace feel better.

"I just want to get away," Grace had mumbled. Between the pressure at work and her frustrations and discouragement with querying her book, she wanted to escape. A new idea had struck that night, and when Grace proposed getting away to write it, Mom and Dad offered to give Grace her Christmas present early.

Her phone released a jolly ringtone, festive and fitting of the holiday season. Grace waved goodbye to her Uber driver and swiped to answer.

"Hi, Mom."

"Did you make it yet, sweetie?"

"Just barely."

"And?"

Mom had suggested Jackson Hole and been in full support of a writing getaway, but the minute she learned Grace's timetable for the trip, Mom had immediately begun to complain about her leaving during Christmas. It was bad enough, Mom had claimed, that Grace's sister, Stephanie, would be unable to come home for the holiday, with Stephanie's husband being stationed in Florida. To have Grace gone too would feel too much like an empty nest.

Grace did feel bad leaving her parents to celebrate alone. Still, this was the only extended break Grace had from her job at Halveics Wellness, where they offered essential oils, whole medicine alternatives, gentle cleaning products, and the like, via phone and online orders.

Grace had gone on plenty of writing retreats with friends, but every time she'd gotten precious little actual writing done.

While fun getaways, time was usually spent chatting with her friends instead of writing. She needed some way to awaken her sleeping muse. It had to be now.

Mom had said she'd understood and, with some coercion from Grace's dad, relented to Grace's timeframe.

"Just got to the inn," Grace said. "It's beautiful here."

"Are you in love?"

"Absolutely. Montana and I are getting married."

"Perfect. I was hoping to plan a wedding this summer," Mom said with a laugh. "Seriously, though, how is it?"

"It's...nice." Grace couldn't give much more detail than that. Not when she hadn't seen much beyond the snow-capped trees.

"That's good. So you'll write what you need to and skedaddle on back home by Christmas, right?"

Grace laughed. "Mom," she reprimanded. They'd gone over this. Today was Tuesday. Grace's stay was booked for a week, and Christmas Day, Friday, happened to fall right in the middle of that week. Grace was a grown woman and Mom had to accept that sometimes her kids wouldn't be home for Christmas.

"I know," Mom said with resignation. "And you know I fully support what you're doing. It's just, now that you're gone...it won't be the same without you here for Christmas. Uncle Mike will be here—he'll wonder where you are."

Grace loved her mom's only brother. When she was little, Uncle Mike had been a human jungle gym, and then as she'd grown up, he'd been a fierce contender on Mario Kart and a shoulder to cry on. Grace hadn't seen him in a few months, but she'd weighed this fact ahead of time and knew Uncle Mike would want her to have her trip.

"He sees me on social media, Mom."

"You know, it really is too bad you left. He told me last night he's bringing his associate, that one I told you about. The one who just got divorced. Terry something."

Grace pinched the bridge of her nose. Her mom's unexpected guilt trip was completely ruining the inn's serenity. She wasn't about to call her Uber driver back and board the plane. Nor did she want to reschedule her flight and leave here a minute before she planned to. Not when she hadn't done what she came here to do.

Sure, she wanted to be with her family for Christmas, but she saw them all the time as it was. This was her Christmas present, and Mom was ruining it.

"I've got to get out of the road, there's another car coming," Grace lied, gazing down the absent, snowy lane the Uber driver had taken once he'd dropped her off. "I'll talk to you later, okay?"

"I'm sure there's still time for you to reschedule your flight," Mom said, ignoring her. "Get some writing done, come home Christmas Eve. Win-win!"

"Bye, Mom."

Grace hung up before Mom could say anything else. Work was stressful enough. It was hard to work a dead-end job at a call center when her heart was in writing. She intended on making enough money with her stories to quit her job, but scribbling away on napkins during lunchtime and writing on weekends wasn't cutting it.

This was her chance. The idea she'd adapted for a story of a fantasy romance between a woman who could wield magic and a man who'd been raised by trees in the American wasteland was going to be a bestseller. The idea was catchy and thriving. She had the perfect tagline. Her brain was bursting with ideas and conversations and all she needed was the time to craft the story the way it was acting out in her mind. To *live* in the world she was trying to create.

This story would be the one. It was unique enough. She was sure no agent had represented anything like it. If she gave the story everything she had, immersed herself in the world she hoped to create, she couldn't fail.

Or at least that was what she told herself.

While Mom supported her writing, Grace knew Mom wanted her to stop living in her own head. Now that Grace had graduated from college and obtained a degree in literature that did her little good in finding a job other than the one Grace had been working at since high school, Mom thought Grace needed to find a man who could ground her in reality. Help her grow up and adult or something. But Grace didn't want reality—not when made-up men were so much better than those in real life. Besides, she'd already moved into her own place last year. Wasn't that adult enough?

Bells tinkled in the distance, and a horse-drawn sleigh jangled its way toward a quintessential red barn situated feet away from the inn. A man in a cowboy hat and a thick wool coat held the reins, clicking his teeth for the gray-and-white-splotched horse to slow.

"That's not something you see every day," she muttered, falling in love with the scenery all over again.

Hoping to recapture the relief she'd felt before the phone call, Grace attempted to wheel her suitcase toward Harper's Inn. Snow clumped along the wheels, making it practically impossible for her to drag her suitcase. She ended up carrying it the old-fashioned way up the stairs, along the shoveled sidewalk and to the entrance, a white door marked by multiple windowpanes.

A louder bell chimed to announce her entrance. The cheery smell of cinnamon and cloves swirled through her nostrils. Grace inhaled, allowing the aroma to settle through her senses. She stomped snow from her boots and shook snowdrops from her blonde hair.

"Hello, there," said a friendly woman from behind a counter.

Her long brown hair was twined in two braids that hung behind her back. She was young, close to Grace's twenty-two years, she would guess, and she wore a cozy red sweater with a white collar folded over from beneath. "Welcome to Harper's Inn."

Grace glanced around the inn's cozy entryway. Tile covered only a square of space in the opening where a coatrack stood like a tree without leaves beside a full-length mirror lined with twinkle lights. To the left, an intimate living room staged to look like the parlor of a time long past hosted a towering Christmas tree smothered with emerald green tulle and fat red bulbs. Perfectly wrapped presents created small mountains at the tree's base. A handful of overstuffed armchairs were positioned around a snapping fireplace.

"That settles it," Grace said, smiling with absolute contentment. "I'm never leaving."

The woman behind the counter smiled back. "That's what we like to hear. Do you have a reservation? I'm afraid we're fully booked through the holidays."

Grace shook more snow from her hair. She'd heard the inn was typically full for at least a year in advance, but to her surprise, there had been an opening when she'd gone online to get a reservation. "Yes, under Grace Eastland."

The woman scanned her device on its dock, pausing with a pleased grin. "There you are! Welcome. I'm Juniper Harper. My parents own this place, and I go by Junie, since the double 'pers' in my name sound weird."

Grace laughed. She liked this woman already. "Hi, Junie. You live here then?"

"I do, and I love it."

"I can't say I blame you for that." Grace glanced toward the narrow hall leading past the welcome desk, catching sight of a dining area at its end.

"You're all checked in, Grace," Junie said, plucking a set of keys from a hook on the wall behind her. "Here are your keys. You're upstairs, in room eleven."

"That's my lucky number," Grace said.

"Lucky you got that room then." Junie grinned. "I'm sure I'll see you around."

"Thanks." Grace took the keys, but she wasn't quite ready to head upstairs just yet. She wanted to soak in the surroundings down here for a little longer. Maybe it was the writer in her, but she loved details; she loved the square trim along the corners of every doorframe, and the stained-glass montage situated above the entry into the front room.

Only a few people loitered. A woman holding a small terrier in one arm was attempting to coerce her young daughter from the room with her free hand.

"Hang on," the little girl said, eyeing something on the table across from the fireplace. "Look at this."

Grace wheeled her suitcase through the entrance, taking advantage of its opening before mother and daughter exited. She gazed in wonder at the lined wallpaper climbing from white wainscoting. A painting of the forest in summer featured a small cottage built of stone and climbing with ivy. It was quaint and picturesque and held an otherworldly feel to it that she was instantly sure she wanted in her book.

Grace moved in for a closer look. She inspected the shadows pooling beneath branches and the light casted from a break in the clouds overhead; gentle, consistent brushstrokes left their mark to craft such a mesmerizing scene. Even the details in the edifice's stone sides were a wonder. A small golden plate beneath the frame labeled it, "The Homestead."

She had the urge to go Mary Poppins on this painting, to dive right in and explore.

Behind her, the mom reprimanded her daughter in an exasperated tone, pulling Grace from her reverie. "No, no, Evie. Don't touch things we can never replace."

"I'm just looking," the little girl replied.

Curiosity got the better of her, and Grace's attention was drawn to the same thing the little girl referenced. Among a collection of old dishes and floral, hand-painted teacups poised on a metal stand, an antique radio stood like a tower on a sea of lace.

The young girl fiddled with the radio's two front knobs like she was drawing on an Etch-a-Sketch. Her mom bustled over, curly-haired dog in hand with the other outstretched. "Evie, I said don't touch."

The young girl lowered her hand. Dark hair tufted out beneath a red beanie. "What is it?" she asked. At the same moment, a man in a cowboy hat entered the room. Snow gathered at his boot soles, and a pair of thick gloves stuck out from the pockets of his wool-lined coat. Was he the same man Grace had seen driving the sleigh before she'd come inside?

"I think it's an old radio," her mother said. "Now come on. We should have left ten minutes ago."

"That's not just any radio." The cowboy removed his hat, giving Grace a full-fledged view of his rugged jawline and pink-tinged cheeks speckled with a day's growth. Her temperature rose a few notches.

"It's not?" The girl raised a brow. "How come?"

The man's expressions were fascinating. Grace examined the intricate way his brow twitched, the way humor played on his attractive mouth, the way he maintained a grip on the crown of his hat with only three fingers. "Rumor has it this radio once belonged to Santa Claus."

Grace's brows lifted. That was the last thing she'd expected him to say. Curiosity got the better of her, and she waited for him to continue.

2

The little girl's thoughts were along the same wavelength. Her face pinched, showcasing just how full her lower lip was. "No, it didn't!"

"It did," the cowboy said. "My grandpa worked here when Miss Junie's grandma turned this place into an inn. He told me the story."

"What story?" the girl asked.

He crouched before the girl, rested a hand on the table in front of the radio, and one of his knees touched the carpet. The girl kept her gaze plastered to the charmer. Her youthful blue eyes were completely fixated on him. Grace took the girl's cue and pegged her attention to his handsome face—the flicker of delight in his brown eyes, and the mischievous lilt to his lips.

"A hundred years ago, Santa forgot to stop by here Christmas Eve," he said.

The girl's mother stroked her dog, opening her mouth as if wanting to interrupt. Clearly, she was conflicted. Probably the same way Grace was—filled with enough nosiness about the radio to let him keep talking.

The girl folded her arms. "Santa wouldn't forget anyone."

"Oh, but he did," said the cowboy. "My grandpa told me he got no presents that year. And Santa, he just felt awful. Just after Christmas, Santa came by with this radio as a way to make up for the slip."

Second by second, stardust fell into the girl's eyes. Her smile spread, revealing perfect tiny teeth, and excitement descended on her as though an egg filled with sparkles had cracked over her head. "Really? This was really Santa's?"

"Really." The cowboy's smile was made of charm. Grace was enthralled by his ability to weave a tale in mere minutes that was captivating enough to keep three women enchanted this long.

"What a nice fairy tale," the mom said from behind him, though she didn't sound like it was nice at all. Her cynicism broke the enchantment of his words. Hmm. Apparently, she wasn't as dazzled by his story as Grace and the little girl. Hardness struck behind her eyes, and Grace wondered if this was a mom who opted not to indulge in childhood fantasies like Santa Claus and the Tooth Fairy. If that was the case, whoever this cowboy was, he'd just made things a whole lot harder for her.

"It's not a fairy tale, ma'am," the cowboy said.

Her lips pinched out a smile. "And let me guess, it only plays Christmas carols." She waved a hand toward the radio.

"Oh no." He rose and faced her, returning the wide-brimmed hat to his head. "I've never heard a single tune come from it, and I've worked here for years."

"Then why keep it?" the little girl asked.

"Why not?"

The three of them turned to face Grace. Heat blushed on her cheeks. Enthralled as she was by it, she'd never meant to enter their conversation. The question slipped out on its own.

A flash of irritation crossed the cowboy's expression, which was an abrupt change compared to the easy way he'd interacted with the young girl.

She had their attention now. Might as well finish her thought.

Grace ignored him and directed her question at the child. "If you had a radio that Santa himself brought for you, wouldn't you keep it too?"

The girl wrinkled her nose. "My mom says we get rid of things we don't use."

Her mom's lips bobbed as if wanting to pose another argument, but the cowboy spoke first. "Your mom is a wise lady," he said.

The mom's face hardened, combatting the smile she failed to keep in place. She adjusted the dog in her arms and waved to her daughter. "Come on, sweetie. We've taken up too much of this nice man's time."

"Not at all," the cowboy said. The little girl obviously wanted to continue talking to him, but she dutifully placed her gloved hand in her mother's and walked to the inn's door. She gave the cowboy a final, wistful glance before the bell tinkled their exit.

The cowboy bent at the waist as if engaging the radio in a stare-down. Grace brushed aside the unexpected appreciation of his back pockets, gathered her courage, and wheeled her suitcase to stand beside him. "You had that little girl wrapped around your finger," she said.

The cowboy straightened and rested a hand on his hip. His eyes were chocolate brown, his proximity had the warm tone of firesides and cuddle blankets, and a lock of dark hair swept across his forehead beneath the brim of his hat.

Grace's breath hitched under the full force of his gaze. A sideline profile view had been enough to draw her in, but his shoulders, his tall stance, the effect his features had on her ability to take in a full breath was more than she anticipated. She legitimately trembled in her boots and had to swallow.

"I did, didn't I?" His expression wasn't nearly as warm as it had been. No smile, and his eyes were guarded. Grace could sense him building an invisible wall between them as if to maintain his distance. Clearly, he wasn't as interested in talking to her as she was to him. Without another word, he tapped the brim of his hat and turned to leave.

Grace would never have continued to pester a man who so obviously didn't want to talk, but he'd just made a claim she couldn't ignore. Before he took more than two steps, she called to him. "Okay, spill. Where did the radio really come from?"

He faced her again. The twinkle left his eyes. "I was telling the truth," he said.

"Not possible."

"You don't believe in Santa Claus, Miss..."

"I'm Grace Eastland. And no, I don't believe in Santa anymore."

The same irritation that had flashed across his eyes earlier made a reappearance. He lifted his chin; his body went rigid. "Pity," he said.

Heat filled Grace's cheeks. This man was tying her up in red knots brighter than those on the presents staged around the sitting room's beguiling Christmas tree. Was he really that bothered she didn't believe in Santa Claus or was it something else?

She waited for him to apologize for his rudeness or even introduce himself. He did neither, and as there was no way to salvage this botched conversation, she gripped her suitcase handle and prepared to roll past him to find her room.

Somewhere in the vicinity of the reception desk, Junie cleared her throat. The man peered at her, muttered under his breath, and then turned back to Grace.

"Sorry," he said, offering a hand as though he'd just remembered what manners were. "I'm Boone Harper."

If just looking at him had this much of an impact on her, Grace wasn't sure she'd be able to recover from a little handshake. She had to admit, his appeal lessened slightly after the way he was treating her. Inhaling, she slipped her fingers into his. He had a steady grip, and the calluses on his hands brushing her palms weren't exactly unpleasant. Cowboy, indeed.

"Harper? Is that what brings you to Harper's Cottage?" Grace gave another attempt at civility. She retrieved her hand before she sustained any burns.

"I work here," he said. "I told you I was telling the truth. My grandpa was Junie's grandma's cousin. He started working here with the horses and it's become a family trade."

"Oh, you take care of the horses here?" So he *was* the man she'd seen driving the sleigh toward the barn earlier.

"That I do."

Horse-drawn sleigh rides were one of the prominent features offered in the pamphlet for the inn. Grace had hoped to schedule one. Could be good book research, which was exactly why she was here.

Except how lame would that make her, to request a solo ride in a sleigh? She had no one to sidle up in that sleigh with. Not that having a date was a requirement, but still. It would make her singleness more than obvious.

Then again, that wasn't necessarily a bad thing...

A couple shuffled past her. She inched forward to avoid a collision, closer to the table and, inadvertently, closer to Boone. He might as well have been another fire for all the heat seeping off of him. Grace's heart rate kicked up a few notches. When was the last time a man had this kind of impact on her?

Um, never.

She had a sudden desire to keep the conversation going. Without really knowing exactly what to say, she cleared her throat.

"How do you turn it on?"

"Excuse me?"

More of that heat slammed into her cheeks. "The radio! I meant the radio." She gestured clumsily toward the old tower, cursing herself the entire time. How do you turn it on? Come on. Talk about horrible pickup lines.

Boone had mastered the sideways grin. His lips tugged upward along one side, and a dimple peeked out, though it vanished just as quickly as it came. Someone kill her now. The man had a dimple.

"You're welcome to fiddle with it but the radio never plays. I'm not sure it's even plugged in anymore. Now it's only decoration."

Instead of standing there and risking getting swept under the weight of his penetrating gaze, Grace reached for the left knob. She imagined a time long past, a time before television and cell phones, when families would gather to listen to stories being played out on radios just like this one, to news broadcasts and war updates.

"Hard to believe this thing is a hundred years old," he said, his long fingers accompanying Grace's to turn the other knob.

"Yeah," she said, not really hearing *what* he said. She could only focus on his hand and how close it was to hers. Good King Wenceslas, he was unraveling her a thread at a time and they'd only just met.

"Well." Boone drew his hand away and tipped his hat toward her. He backed a few steps away, and the space allowed her body to cool instantly. "I have to get going, but it was nice to meet you."

Bashful in a way she wasn't usually, Grace tucked her arms closer to her body and folded a hair behind her ear. "You too, Boone." Boone. Just saying his name added another log to the fire flickering inside her.

Her writer's mind drew up the word's definition in an instant. She'd always had that problem, never able to separate names of things from what—or who—they represented. A boon was something that was helpful or a blessing to someone else. If he turned out to be anything like his name, she wasn't sure she could handle it.

"You have a good day." He strolled toward the reception desk.

Grace watched him talk to Junie for several minutes, and then, realizing she was staring, clicked up her suitcase handle and sauntered past to find her way to her room.

3

———

Boone tromped down the snowy steps, eager to get back out to the barn, back out to where horses awaited and where women stopped trying to interfere in his life. Before he made it halfway down the porch steps, the bell rang behind him and Junie stepped outside, hugging her arms tight around her.

"What are you doing, Junie?" he asked, turning enough to prop one boot on the step above. He wasn't exactly happy with her at the moment. She continued to pester him about being nice to the guests. He hoped whoever the woman in the living room was—Grace. Oh man, *Grace*—hadn't heard Junie clear her throat at him.

She was his cousin, not his mother. But she was also, technically, his employer. At that moment, he'd decided to look at things in that way. So he'd been civil. And then he'd walked away at the first opportunity.

Giving the guests—especially the female guests—more attention often led them in a direction he had no intention of going. He couldn't count the number of times women had asked Junie for Boone's contact information before leaving the inn.

He'd also made it perfectly clear he was done talking to Grace, but she kept right on with her questions. Granted, the idea of a radio belonging to Santa Claus would make anyone question him, but still. She could have asked Junie what she wanted to know, not him.

"I just got a call from Troy," Junie said. "His dad's injured."

Boone's gaze flicked in the direction of the barn. That wasn't good. Their other sleigh driver, Troy, sometimes had his dad fill in when they needed him to. That need didn't happen often, but Christmas was coming in three more days.

"Injured? How?" Boone asked.

"He was carrying something for his wife into their basement and slipped on the stairs. He's going in for hip surgery this afternoon."

A fall down the stairs at his age? Troy's father, Rick, was old enough to be any of their grandfathers. "What about his wife? Is she okay?"

Junie's lower jaw began to quiver from the frosty, ten degree morning, but she shuffled toward the top step. "She's all right. I've offered to go help, but their daughter lives close by, and Troy said they'll be okay."

"Thanks for telling me. I'll be sure to stop by after the surgery. Maybe we can bring them some dinner from the kitchens."

"I thought so too. And Boone...?"

Boone knew what Junie would be getting at. He hurried to ward her off before she could ask. "We'll find someone else," he said, turning to continue his trek down to the cleared sidewalk.

Junie trundled down the steps toward him. Boone dropped his mouth in mock surprise. "What are you doing, Junie? Leaving the reception desk unmanned? Shocking."

She slugged him. "The reception desk will be fine for a few minutes. Our inn won't, at least not for our annual ride up the mountain Christmas Eve. Sure, Troy will still be here to drive, but you know one sleigh won't carry all of our guests. Can't you forget your bitterness for one year and help me out? Finding a replacement sleigh driver isn't as easy as you think."

"I would know," Boone grumbled. "Since I'm the one who will be finding the replacement."

"Come on. Please? All you have to do is drive the guests up to the peak. The bonfire will already be in place. The cocoa stand will be all ready to go. Mom and I will be the ones talking about 'the event' a hundred years ago. You won't even have to talk to anyone. Just wait in the sleigh with the horses as your only company. I know that's your favorite way to spend your time."

As a matter of fact, he had once liked the annual sleigh ride to the mountain peak for a bonfire and to hear the story of the inn's origins. His mom and Junie's had been close. They'd been the one to start the tradition of a bonfire with the guests who opted to stay over Christmas. Guests all piled into their bigger sleighs and were carted up the mountainside where a large bonfire awaited. A hot cocoa stand and set of porta potties was on hand. Guests drank cocoa, mingled near the fire's warmth, and then Junie or her mother—or both women—took turns telling the tale of when Santa made his notorious visit.

Laughter and joy were rampant. Guests returned year after year for a repeat of the occasion. Boone had joined in with the rest of them, laughing and singing the carols the guests instigated during the sleigh ride. Until his wife passed away.

Even the thought of Amy now stabbed him straight in the heart. The memory of her death made air for breathing hard enough to come by as it was. But Christmas only thinned the air that much more. Enduring the holiday was like climbing Mount Everest without any gear or oxygen. His head went light and began pounding. Fatigue washed over him, and nausea at the thought of exactly what he'd lost when his wife had died rendered him unable to do much more than exist.

"Horses are my favorite way of spending my time," he said, forcing a smile. He took too long to reply, and he knew it.

"Come on, Boone," Junie said, elevating her voice. "You know Laura just quit and Sam is on vacation with her family. I'm so short-staffed, it's not even funny, and now we won't have enough drivers? I need you."

He refused to let her plea get to him. They still had time, and there were plenty of horsemen down in the town who could hold reins and drive a team up the mountain. "I'm sorry, Junie, but you know I can't do it. We have enough notice. We can find someone else."

Junie opened her mouth to argue, but he inclined his head at his cousin and began the trek through the snow toward the large red barn.

Childhood memories of romping through this mountainside, of herding his grandparents' sheep and his first horseback rides with his father, of traipsing along with Junie and her sister, Bella, to gather wildflowers and the time Junie fell into a beaver dam, were rampant in his mind.

One memory he didn't have of this place was of his late wife, Amy, or their unborn child who'd died in the womb. He'd never gotten to hold that child, not even after the accident. Thoughts of them both now pricked his eyes.

Boone blinked them away, remembering how after high school he'd left the inn to work on a ranch. Amy had flirted her way into his life. She'd been a down-to-earth woman who worked at the same ranch he did, and their relationship quickly built on a mutual love for farm life and sunsets and swings on apple trees.

Since her death, his heart hadn't beat the same. He was amazed it could keep on beating at all, if he were being honest with himself. He'd lost a part of himself with her. That was the reason he'd come back to Grandma Harper's. The prospect of living at his family's old cottage had been welcome. Secluded as he was here, surrounded by antiques and things that didn't and would never belong to him, he could let go of as many memories of Amy as he could.

So he'd left everything behind in Deer Lodge. He'd brought only the clothes on his back. Furniture, clothes, the baby things Amy had been collecting for eight months before she'd died had all been abandoned. The only thing he kept that belonged to him now were some old awards from his rodeo days and Amy's favorite sweater. It had long since lost her smell. Even now, he considered getting rid of it as well, but she'd worn that the day before she'd died. He wasn't ready to let it go along with the rest of her things.

Every woman reminded him of Amy in some way. The way they tossed their hair. The way they carried themselves. He'd worked to immunize himself against any other woman's appeal since he lost Amy.

But the woman he'd spoken with near the radio wouldn't leave his mind. Or rather, her name wouldn't leave his mind. Grace. He pressed his eyes closed and shook away the sting her name alone brought.

She was beautiful, there was no denying that. His heart had sparked for the first time in years, adding an extra beat the minute he allowed himself to meet her blue eyes. That hadn't happened in so long, but he had done his best to ignore the sensation. To ignore her.

He'd been ready to walk away until Junie had to go and clear her throat. And then he'd learned the woman's name.

Grace.

Tears stung his eyes as he entered the large red barn. He blinked hard, stepped across the scattered bits of straw, and

reached for Hazelnut's brush. The horse responded to his proximity, hooves prancing in place as he stood beside her. Grace. He
had to avoid that woman as much as possible.

"Hey, girl," he said, running the brush along her
mane. Hazelnut's black eye gave him a sideways
glance, and he hugged his free arm around her,
resting his head against her. Horses had always been calming to
him, which was another reason he'd opted to come back to
Grandma Harper's after the accident. Junie was right—being in
the barn, with the horses, away from people, was where he
preferred.

He could tease children easily and enjoyed the delight they
often got from the story of the radio. He even enjoyed talking
with guests and families during sleigh rides, which was the
only interaction he had with people these days, really. But
when it came down to Christmas, he wanted—needed—to be
alone. Away from the crowds, away from the music, away from
the smiling and the happiness he knew he could never have
again.

Boone should have known better than to go into the radio's
history with so many people in the room to overhear. Telling the
little girl had been safe enough, or so he'd thought. Though he
would never admit as much out loud, his reservations also
sprang from the part of the radio's history that only he, Junie,
and her mom knew much about:

The radio hadn't played in a hundred years, but when it had,
the guests hadn't just heard music. That music from Santa's
radio had interfered with people's lives. Or so their grandparents
had said.

"We had near to twenty weddings at the inn that next year,"
Grandma had joked. "That's what we get for Santa knowing

what we're all up to all the time. He knew just who to have the radio play for."

According to Grandma Harper, the radio wouldn't respond when someone turned the dial like a normal radio did. Since Santa himself had delivered it to Boone's grandfather, the story went that the radio *chose* who it would play for and when. And when it played, it created havoc for whoever heard the songs. Aunt Meg teasingly called the radio a matchmaker.

Boone and Junie had heard their whole lives about the first year Santa had brought the radio, and how the men and women who had heard the radio play ended up getting together one way or another. He'd learned the hard way not to share that part of the story, especially not around women. Their flirting always picked up a notch whenever he had, as though they thought he was coming on to them.

Junie and Aunt Meg loved to ramble on and on about the romantic notion of the radio being a matchmaker during their annual bonfire, which was another reason Boone refused to take guests up the mountain. He wasn't sure he believed that part of things, especially since none of them—Junie, Aunt Meg, nor him—had ever heard a single note come from it.

Hazelnut released a chuff. Boone straightened, brushed away all thoughts of a meddling, matchmaking antique radio, and patted her side. No, he meant what he'd told Junie. He would do what he'd done for the past three years. He would stay as far away from people as he could until Christmas was over.

"Besides, how can I leave you all alone?" he said to Hazelnut, though he knew how stupid it sounded. Still, he glanced around at the larger sleighs parked in the barn's open space across from the horse stalls. The single sleigh was missing from its spot. Troy would be returning with his customers soon. Boone would be sure to ask after his father once he did.

On that note, Boone pulled his cell phone from his pocket

and began scrolling through his contacts in search of a replacement sleigh driver. They would find someone else to help. He couldn't do it.

Christmas would come and go this year, just like it did every year. And Boone would wait for the holiday to pass, praying like always that the pain of memory would pass right along with it.

4

Grace sat at the edge of her bed, notebook open, pen poised, and attempted to recreate with words the exact shape of Boone's jawline and the molten chocolate color of his eyes which were framed by dark lashes. No—not framed. Bordered. No, that wasn't right either. Emphasized? Ugh, she wasn't getting anywhere with this.

She shook her head and inhaled, ready to invoke the inn's tantalizing cinnamon scent that had trickled its way into her completely heartwarming room with its white walls, dark wood ceilings, matching dark wood doors leading to a balcony outside and an adjoining bathroom. She could have sat in the plush, white armchair with its massive pink blooms shouting all over the fabric, but she preferred to sit on the bed and enjoy the view of the chair instead.

Time to try again. Grace closed her eyes. Boone had made her mouth water as though sugary, homemade icing were melting on her tongue. Yeah, that was a good one. She leveled the pen, but for some reason, it wouldn't move.

"Oh, come on," she grumbled to the blank page. "He would make the perfect hero in any story." And he would. How any woman could be in the same room with him and not completely salivate over his right-hook smile and impactful gaze was beyond her. She'd come to Harper's Inn for book research, and *wowie* had she gotten it. Boone was definitely book boyfriend material.

Grace lowered the pen with that thought. He wasn't just book boyfriend material. For some reason, she had a hard time capturing the effect he'd had on her on the page. The truth was, Grace hadn't felt what Boone had made her feel in a long time, and she didn't want to trivialize that.

With a man like Boone Harper, she wanted him to be anything but fictional.

But he'd been such a contradiction. Flirtatious and charming one minute and bordering on rudeness the next. Maybe he was married, and he thought she was coming on to him. Had she, though? Grace questioned herself with a saltshaker's worth of chagrin. Here she was mooning over his rating on the gorgeousness scale, and he was probably already taken.

She kept replaying different ways the scenario could have gone downstairs. Her favorite one featured Boone being as completely struck by her as she was by him. They were the only two in the room. He'd asked for her number and then planned a clandestine meeting place where he then swept her into his manly, muscular arms. Hearts throbbing, blood pulsing, he slammed his lips to hers and stole what was left of her breath...

"Snap out of it," Grace chided herself. No such thing had happened with him or would happen. Ever. In frustration, she tossed the notebook and its pencil onto the bed's white duvet and slumped against the pillows.

Of course he was already married. She couldn't figure out why else he'd gone so rigid and acted almost repulsed when she told him her name. When she'd said she didn't believe in Santa Claus.

"Does *anyone* over the age of ten still believe in Santa Claus?" she mused aloud.

A chiming dusted through the air, distilling softly around her like snowfall. The musical sound stroked the base of her neck and sent chills down the backs of her arms in a not-entirely-unpleasant way. Grace perked up at the sound and glanced around the room.

"What was that?" she asked.

Her phone was where she'd placed it on the nightstand. Nothing was playing from it. An old-fashioned alarm clock with a face instead of digital red numbers sat beside the lamp. The TV mounted on the wall above a dresser across from her bed stared back at her with its black screen.

Grace wanted to shrug the tinkling music off like it had been in her imagination, but it sounded too real. Curious, Grace inspected the space, peeking below the bed, lifting the white covers. She opened the door leading out onto the balcony and instantly regretted it when a flurry of frigid air slipped inside. A quick glance in the bathroom showed nothing amiss. Last of all, she checked the closet.

The space was small. She'd laid out a few of her things so they didn't get wrinkled inside her suitcase, but the majority of shelves were bare. Grace stepped in but stopped when her foot met with something spiny.

"Ow!" She lifted her foot. A simple silver chain with an unre- markable pendant dangling from it was strung on the floor. Grace bent and picked the necklace up. "Where did this come from?" She supposed it was left by the previous guest.

Someone knocked on the door. Hurriedly, Grace tucked the chain into her jeans pocket and answered.

Junie beamed in the threshold. Though her hair frizzed along its part on the top of her head and she looked a bit more tired than she had when Grace had first arrived, light still dazzled in her eyes. Grace had the impression Junie was the kind of person who was happy no matter what. She wondered what exactly her duties here at the inn were.

"Hey, there," Junie said. "I'm sorry to bother you, but I am ridiculously short-staffed and wanted to make sure all the guests have plenty of towels. Much to my embarrassment, I'm not sure your room got stocked before you arrived."

"Oh, sure," Grace said, stepping aside for Junie to enter.

"Thanks," Junie said, making her way to the bathroom. She raised her voice to keep right on speaking even though she wasn't directly looking at Grace. "I won't be but a minute. Ordinarily, we have people who clean the rooms and make sure everything is in order, but this time of year is just crazy. I've had two people up and quit on me in the last month, can you believe that?"

"That sucks," Grace said, moving closer so she didn't have to yell. She leaned against the bathroom's doorjamb. "So you own the inn? A guy I met downstairs said your grandparents ran it or something?"

Junie placed a new box of Kleenex in an opening beneath the sink and removed an empty one. Straightening, she brushed the back of her hand against her forehead. "You mean Boone? He's my second cousin. Our grandparents were cousins and they worked together here. So yeah, I've kind of inherited responsibility for this place, you could say, along with my mom. Most of the time I love it, but this year..."

She stepped out of the bathroom, a bright smile on her face. Something told Grace smiling was a natural thing for Junie; even as she spoke of being overwhelmed, she was smiling. "It's pretty incredible, being away from the hubbub and fast pace everywhere else. I went into Salt Lake City once and all those buildings and people and smog?" She inhaled. "Give me the open air any day."

"I get that," Grace said with a little laugh. "I've lived in the city my whole life. This is my first venture into the back country, I guess." Truth be told, it was her first time venturing off on her own, period. Usually, she traveled with at least one other person.

Junie laughed, and the expression lit up a few freckles dusting across her nose. "Back country is about right. Well, I'd better get going. Have a good night."

"Thanks, you too," Grace said. Before she knew it, Junie was out and closing the door behind her. Too late, Grace remembered the necklace she'd found. She should have asked Junie if they had a lost and found of any kind around here.

She found she'd wanted to ask about Boone too. Why he'd been so friendly one minute and so closed off the next. Maybe that would make her interest in him too obvious.

Hold everything. What was she thinking? Her *interest* in him? She was here to write, not moon over the hotel staff. The clock beside her bed ticked, as if reminding her of how much time was passing with every second she wasn't writing.

"It's not like I can force out the words," she grumbled to it.

A few voices rumbled from the hallway outside her door. Someone mentioned something about dinner. Sure enough, the scent of freshly baked rolls tantalized her stomach.

"That settles it," she said. She could always think better when she had something to eat. Might as well head down for some dinner.

Grace retrieved her phone from the nightstand, tucked her room key into her other pocket, and ventured out into the hall. Another woman stepped out from the door across the hall. She looked to be about Grace's age, had a thin nose, auburn hair pooling to her shoulders, and was staring at her phone. She lowered the device long enough to give Grace a friendly smile.

"Hey, there," the woman said. "Dinner smells amazing, doesn't it?" She drew in a long inhale and added another smile.

"It really does," Grace said. In fact, another one of the inn's selling points was the quality of exquisite food served by an on-hand chef.

"Maybe I'll see you down there," the woman said before heading toward the stairs.

"Sounds great," Grace said, waiting a few seconds before taking the same direction.

At the bottom of the stairs, Grace paused. Night had descended early. Darkness flooded the living room, making the lights on the Christmas tree shine that much brighter. Wanting just one quick peek into what she considered her favorite room at this inn, Grace veered toward it.

Muted light still crackled from the fireplace, adding warmth and a sense of cozy secrets to the room, as though these walls had witnessed more than their fair share of stories. And considering the story Boone had shared earlier, that was saying something.

But Santa wasn't real, and the radio was probably just a family heirloom. In any case, the fire welcomed her to sit in the nearest armchair and start typing. She made a mental note to bring her laptop down after dinner.

Heavy footfalls approached and then Boone appeared from the shadows with a cut log in each hand. Grace's heart leapt at the sight of him. She fisted her hands to keep from touching her chest. What was her problem?

He barely glanced her way as he muttered a hasty, "Evening."

"Hey," she said, tucking a strand of hair behind her ear. Her eyes plastered to his movements as he crouched before the fire and tossed the beams onto the pile. He was built better looking than most men, in a stop-and-stare kind of way, the way that made single women do a double take and married women force their gazes away to keep their attention where it belonged. What was he doing driving horse teams in the middle of a Montana wasteland?

He and Junie both mentioned his family had claims staked to this inn. Was that all there was to it?

Boone dusted his hands and lifted his gaze to hers. Grace had been caught staring, but she wasn't about to try and hide that fact. Something about him was magnetic.

A line appeared between his brows. He inclined his head at her. "You have a good evening."

She held out a hand. "Please, don't leave on my account. I didn't mean to interrupt anything." Ugh. What was wrong with her? Please, don't let me interrupt you throwing logs onto the fire? She fought the urge to roll her eyes at herself.

His face remained stoic. "Not interrupting. I just like to make sure the fires stay lit during business hours."

"Right. I was just heading to dinner..." She had the sudden urge to invite him to join her, but if he was this jumpy just being in the same room with her, that probably wouldn't go over well. The two of them did a kind of shuffle, a dance without pre-planned steps. They circled one another, Grace making her way farther in toward the fireplace and Boone circling toward the exit.

"I was just leaving," he said again.

"Are you—" Grace started, when a crackling noise pulled their conversation to a stop. Grace frowned, her attention shifting to the table of antiques on display across the room. Another crackle, and some static followed.

"Was that the radio?" she asked.

Boone's forehead creased. "Impossible."

Grace edged closer to him. He smelled like cinnamon and snowfall. They stood side by side, shoulders touching, hearts pounding as another whirring, crackling sound emitted from the radio.

"I thought you said it didn't work," she said.

He glared at the table. "It doesn't."

"Then where's the sound coming from?"

"I don't know." He crouched to his hands and knees and lifted the lace tablecloth to peer beneath the table. Grace did the same. Shoulders brushing, they peered, but there was no sign of a plug in the wall at all. Next, Boone rose to his knees and inspected the radio itself. With some effort, he lifted it to inspect every angle. It wasn't attached to any source at all, and there were certainly no battery receptacles in it.

Fire blazing at their backs, he placed the radio onto the table once more. Almost at once, the whirring sound increased, and the faintest hint of a song began to eke from the antique speakers.

"...I thought I'd take a ride...seated by my side..."

"Is that..." Grace began.

Boone silenced her with a hand, leaning in close, turning his ear toward the sound.

"...Bells...all the way...Oh, what fun it is to ride..."

"That's 'Jingle Bells,'" Grace said.

"Unbelievable." Boone's statement swept chills down her arms. A tinkling sound emerged then, not from the radio, a sound with clinks and jangles. It was metallic and rattling and yet light enough to brush up Grace's spine with all the tickling effect of a feather. Just enough to trigger goosebumps along the base of her neck.

"What was that?" she asked.

"Sounded like it came from the chimney." The minute they turned, the fire that had been blazing moments before was a sweeping gust of smoke and ash.

"Whoa," Boone said. They exchanged a look. "I just added those extra logs. That's impossible."

Chills crept up the backs of Grace's arms. What was going

on? Boone's head turned slowly until his gaze landed on hers. The last time they locked eyes, his had been guarded and distant. Now, she could swim in his expression. The depth in his gaze was so striking, she had to take a step back and exhale.

"How long did you say you've worked here?" she asked.

"Three years, though I grew up here before that."

"And you've never..."

"Never."

Her mind spun like a top, whirling on a point without an end in sight. "I'm not sure it was the radio," she said.

"What else could it have been?"

She spoke in spite of his biting tone. "I heard something similar in my room earlier, you know, music, and when I went looking for its source..." She rifled in her pocket and removed the necklace. "I found this."

Boone's eyes widened. "Where did you get that?"

Startled by his reaction, Grace closed her fist around the necklace. "I just told you, I heard a tinkling melody in my room and then—"

"Here. I'll take it."

"It's yours?"

"Not exactly." He frowned as Grace relented, placing the necklace in his awaiting palm. What was going on? What in the world was bothering him so much?

"Then what—"

Pain lanced through his expression. Wordlessly, with the necklace still in his fist, he reached across the old books with faded spines, and the black and white photographs on display. He gripped the old radio and lifted it once more, this time completely from the table, bumping a few teacups on their stacked stands in the process. And he stormed from the room.

Grace hurried after. "What are you doing?" she asked.

Rather than make for the dining hall, which was filled with

people enjoying the meal she'd come down for, he veered to the right and through a swinging door.

"Getting some answers," he said through his teeth. He didn't wait for her, and this time she didn't follow him the rest of the way down. This was probably a staff-only section of the inn. Maybe his room was down here. Was he putting the radio in his bedroom?

Grace stood with helpless hands in the hall, watching until he kicked open the door on the end with his feet and disappeared inside.

"What just happened?" she asked no one but herself. And of course, she couldn't give herself any answers. Boone's behavior was beyond confusing. All she did was show him the necklace she'd found. Did he think she'd stolen it?

More bizarre than his moodiness was the radio. Grace couldn't buy into the whole Santa story. The radio playing like that was probably just a joke, a prank played by the inn staff. Why else would Boone have gotten so angry and removed it?

That still didn't explain how the fire completely vanished from the fireplace when it'd been at full blaze moments before. Or the complete wonderment in Boone's expression. Either he was a very good actor, or something else was at work here.

5

This old radio was heavier than Boone had expected it to be. With the old set in hand, when Boone didn't see Junie at the reception desk, he marched right past it, past the dining hall, and down to the office she shared with her mom. He wanted this thing out of his sight. He was tempted to bypass the room altogether and make for the chopping block outside where he'd just finished preparing another day's worth of wood for the fires.

But Junie would never forgive him if he destroyed this old thing. The truth was, he'd never forgive himself, and he really only wanted answers anyway.

Junie and Aunt Meg's office was clean and organized, situated with stacks of labeled plastic totes across from Junie's desk, signifying the decorations for the various holidays the inn was festooned for. Boone slammed the radio down a little too hard on the desk beside her computer.

"Easy," Junie said, coming in behind him.

The irritation that had flared at the sight of his late wife's necklace in Grace's hand kicked up his heartbeat all over again.

He hadn't meant to snap at Grace. And he certainly didn't intend to snap at Junie, though he did intend to ask her a few questions.

A few years ago, Junie had stopped by the cottage one evening to bring by some blankets they were replacing when the main inn was being redecorated. She'd come across something Amy had left behind during their last visit and thought it would be helpful to bring that by for Boone to hold onto.

The sight of that necklace undid him. The reminder of Amy made him miss her even more than he already did, and he broke apart, shattering into a misfit pile of heartbeats. He wilted, his entire body losing its strength because it took everything from him to cry. To accept that Amy was gone and wasn't coming back and that he'd gotten rid of everything the two of them had had together.

He took that locket and tucked it away in a drawer at the cottage. How could the necklace possibly have gotten back to the inn at all, let alone into Grace's hands? Grace, the same woman the radio had played for...

"What's the matter?" Junie asked.

Boone worked to calm himself. He was far too agitated. He inhaled a deep breath and exhaled just as slow, working to keep his voice calm. "Do you know how one of the guests got a hold of this?" With the necklace strung around his middle finger, he allowed it to dangle from his downturned palm and met her eyes, knowing the same recollection passed between them. The day Junie had been a shoulder to cry on when he'd finally allowed himself to grieve Amy's death.

Junie was the one person he could be completely himself with. Again, he worked to steady his frustration.

"Oh, Boone," Junie said. "I thought you had it at the cottage. Were you carrying it around and dropped it somewhere around here?"

"No. It's been tucked away in a drawer at my place."

Junie narrowed her eyes. "Please tell me you're not suggesting what I think you are. Come on, Boone. You can't think I snuck in, stole it, and planted it in one of the guest rooms here."

Even as she spoke the words, he knew his assumption was misplaced. Hearing her say it aloud made him realize just how ludicrous the thought was. Boone rubbed a hand over his face, releasing another breath that allowed his thoughts to clear.

"Sorry," he said, releasing a puff of air. "You're right. It's complete nonsense. I shouldn't have jumped to such a random conclusion." Junie wouldn't do that to him. She wouldn't sneak into his house and rifle through his personal belongings.

She bent for the toolbox below the desk and paused at the sight of the radio beside her computer. "Don't tell me the radio moved its way in here on its own too."

"That was me," he said, resting his hip against the desk.

She hugged the toolbox to her chest. "Uh huh. Care to tell me why you've decided to redecorate?"

"I heard it play, Junie."

He waited for her to deny the admission. To call him an idiot and remind him that the old thing hadn't been heard to play for a hundred years.

But her expression remained unchanged. She tucked her lips into her teeth.

"Why don't you look surprised?" he asked. A thought dawned. He folded his arms. "You've heard it too, haven't you?"

Junie peered to one side and then the other. She lowered the toolbox to the chair, inched forward, and closed the door the rest of the way. The closed door added a layer of privacy. Junie spoke with her back to him.

"I—I admit, I heard it the other night. It only played one day of 'The Twelve Days of Christmas.'"

"And?" Boone asked. No one had heard the radio play—not

even his own mother before she passed away. Now, though Junie's parents were still around, only he and Junie oversaw the inn and its maintenance.

"And ever since then it's played me one verse every day. The sixth day I saw six swans a swimming in the thawed center of West Lake. That couple over there..."

She made her way to the window across from her desk and pointed outside. Boone noticed the couple he'd taken out for a sleigh ride earlier now out in the moonlight, arguing. He almost laughed at the sight. Of course they were arguing. Lacie and Jared had been the most irritated guests he'd taken out in a long time. Usually, when couples wanted to ride together, they, well, wanted to be together. But as these two sat together, they repelled each other like the wrong ends of magnets. Cold and frowning and rigid, and bickering the entire time, and sitting as far as possible from the other.

"What's their story?" he asked. He'd wondered it at the time, but not enough to do much about it.

Junie's warm palm left a moist outline on the window's cold glass. "It's the weirdest thing. They claim not to be married. But when I pull up their reservation on the computer, they have the same last name. The girl, Lacie, seemed completely shocked when I showed her as much. She kept insisting she'd booked her own separate room, not a room with him. You know how fast our rooms fill up. People book a year in advance or more! There's no way she had a room of her own."

"Maybe she's mentally ill," Boone suggested.

"She's not. It's the radio."

Boone wasn't so sure about that. Music may have played from it, but that didn't mean anything. He'd adamantly denied the romantic speculation Junie and Aunt Meg had indulged in since he'd returned to West Hills. "You heard it," he argued. "And it hasn't meddled in your life."

Junie's gaze swept to the door, across from which lay the kitchen entrance. The chef, Mason Devries, in his white hat passed at the same moment. Color pinked up her cheeks enough to let Boone know the answer.

"No way," he said. "You and Mason?"

Junie whirled and slammed her back to the wall. "Shh," Junie said. "Nothing has happened necessarily. Just that every time the radio plays, we're somehow managing to stand in that front room without knowing how we got there. He burned dinner the other night because he didn't remember leaving in the middle of preparing it."

Boone chuckled. "I'm sure the guests loved that."

She rolled her eyes. "He's never had so many complaints about his food. Who am I kidding—he's never had any complaints! That's why we hired Mason Devries, because everything he cooks is delicious. He's crazy frustrated by it."

"Understandably so," Boone said, straightening and resting a hand on the radio. He examined its cherry-wood color and dated design, baffled as to how it could possibly be playing now, a hundred years later, when it never once played in all the time he'd been around.

The music playing from the radio had been the reason his grandparents had turned their home into an inn in the first place. Music began to play shortly after its arrival...and... Again, Boone recalled his mother mentioning the sheer number of weddings they'd hosted that year because of the radio's magic. He attempted to shake his head, to call the notion out as an impossibility.

He wanted to continue denying the matchmaker claim or that he'd heard anything at all, but the memories, the music he'd heard in the room with Grace, resonated too deeply to do anything else at the moment. He wanted to play off Junie's speculation too, to label her as paranoid or making things up, but he'd heard the story behind this radio his whole life. His grandpa had shared what it'd been like for his own father to meet Santa Claus in person, to receive a gift like this from St. Nick himself. Boone had believed it for so long, he'd be a fool to ignore this part of things now.

"So what do we do?" he said. "Send a letter to Santa? Tell him to stop messing with our lives?"

"Is that really what you want for Christmas?"

Her question struck too many chords within him to be ignored. "What does that mean?"

Her face wilted into an apologetic grimace. "Seeing that necklace really got to you when I first brought it over. I can only imagine how you're feeling having it pop up again out of nowhere. Especially when you thought it was tucked away at your cottage."

"I'm fine," he said, hoping she got the hint. He needed her to stop. Now. The radio was *not* the reason that necklace reappeared.

"I know you don't talk about her, Boone, but you've been different since Amy died. What if the radio's magic placed that necklace in this woman's path? To bring the two of you together?"

The same raw, aching emotion he battled every day built up like a blocked drain. It took everything in him to repress how much it hurt to have his wife and unborn daughter gone. Why else did Junie think he'd sequestered himself at the cottage if not to forget? And yet, even there, he couldn't escape his own recollections.

His jaw clenched. "Don't go there."

Junie offered her hands in surrender. "All I'm saying is, it might not hurt to let yourself open up to someone again."

"Not because some magical radio picked a match for me."

"Boone—"

He swept a hand between them, fighting the bitter burning in the corners of his eyes. "No way, Junie. Thank you for your concern, but no. This isn't the time to make hasty decisions, especially ones that could entangle your life with someone else's just because you get swept away in an impulsive moment. We just have to wait this out until Christmas is over. Then our heads will be clear, and this will all go back to normal."

"We?"

"What?"

"You said 'we.'"

"No, I didn't." He sounded too defensive, and he knew it.

Junie gave him a sympathetic, almost piteous smile. "Boone, Mason and I were both in the same room with the radio when it first started playing 'The Twelve Days of Christmas.' I don't know about that couple, Lacie and Jared, but was someone else in the room with you when you heard the radio play?"

"I don't see why that matters." He knew where she was going. He was *not* going to tell Junie that the same woman who'd heard the radio play with him also somehow happened to be holding a distinctive necklace that just happened to belong to his dead wife. Especially not when Junie had speculated as much earlier. He refused to confirm it.

"Evidence is showing that it *does* matter," Junie said. "You deserve another chance at love. At happiness. Maybe the radio knows that."

"It's a *radio*."

The longer they spoke, the angrier he grew. Boone didn't like this side of himself. He didn't realize how quickly anger had become his natural reaction until that moment. He shouldn't be upset at Junie. He knew she was only trying to help. That didn't convince his emotions, however.

"I had my shot," he said softly.

The sadness in Junie's eyes was unbearable. "Boone. I don't think we only get one."

Tears welled in his eyes. He blinked hard and willed them away. "We need to put that thing in the attic until Christmas is over," he said. Then they could go on having normal lives without this accursed holiday interfering. He cradled the radio in his arms once more.

Junie didn't protest as he thought she would. She only said, "I'm sorry."

The apology seemed like it was trying to cover so much. It said so much without specifying. She knew how his heart hurt without Amy. He wasn't sure whether to be reassured by that or bothered that his pain was so transparent.

Either way, he paused at the door long enough to speak over his shoulder. "Me too," he said before exiting and placing the radio up in the darkest corner of the attic.

6

G race peered at the suggested itinerary she'd found on her bedside table the next morning. She'd never been one for doing much yoga or for spending money on spa treatments like massages and pedicures offered at the inn, but she fully intended to yoga and spa it up while she was here. Relaxation and exercise were often the best instigators of her muse. She always got the best ideas, the most interesting character conversations and plot lines while either showering or running.

Harper's Inn was going to be a source of pure inspiration. She could feel it.

Not only that, but the forest was calling. Every time Grace glanced out the windows, the sight of snow spreading from all sides was too engrossing. It was like being on a cruise completely surrounded by ocean, except this was no rocking boat, and she could leave her room to explore the surroundings.

And boy, did she want to go a-roving.

She didn't own a scrap of winter attire, so part of the Christmas present from her parents had been an online shopping spree. Dad was even gracious enough not to give her a hard time for spending so much on items she'd probably never wear again.

"You'll want something warm," Dad had said, clicking on the red puffy coat with the fur-lined hood even though it was twice as much as some of the other offerings online.

"You would know," Grace had said. And he would. Dad viewed winter the way some people might view a medieval torture chamber. He'd grown up in northern Canada and the instant he was old enough to live on his own, Dad had skedaddled down to the southern U.S., to nearly as hot a place as he could find.

His negativity toward the cold and the snow and the icy roads and nostril hairs freezing while standing outside to wait for the school bus to come had only infiltrated, oh, *every* conversation they'd ever had about the season. But he'd always managed to voice his dislike with a laugh and a joke, and for some reason, none of his poor opinions kept Grace from wanting to experience winter herself.

Grace slid the accompanying notepad closer and marked a few of the boxes. "Spa day, definitely," she said, checking the first one. "Ice skating? Not so much." Not without someone to hold onto should she fall. Which she was bound to do. "Ooo, bowling?" She marked that box too, though again, bowling alone wasn't all that appealing.

She wasn't here to bowl. On second thought, she crossed that one out. "I'm here to write," she told herself. The spa day was only to fuel her writing. She had to stay focused on that.

The last box caught her attention with more force than any of the others had done. It read: *Sleigh rides.*

Venture into West Hills' winter wonderland with one of our competent, friendly drivers for an unparalleled view of Montana's rugged, unblemished terrain. With the well-trained horse's breezy bells jingling all the way, see why guests return again and again simply for one of these incomparable winter adventures! Ride solo or with friends. Schedule in the lobby.

A sleigh ride was definitely on her to-do list, and not just because she wanted first-hand experience of what it was like to ride in a horse-drawn sleigh so she could accurately describe the experience in her book. The last time she'd spoken with Boone, he'd been angry with her for having found the necklace. He'd stormed off with the old radio and she hadn't seen it—or him —since.

Schedule in hand, ready to greet the spa and trigger her inner writing genius, Grace slid her feet into her slippers and made her way back down to the reception desk. She darted a quick peek into the living room. Sure enough, the table covered by the lace cloth held only teacups, black and white photographs, and old books. It didn't look the same without the radio there, and the sight without it brought a little pang of sadness inside of Grace.

Mumbling directed her attention back to the reception desk. "Where did that thing go? I could have sworn it was right here. Where's Sam when I need her?" Junie's back was arched behind the tablet serving as the register and she rifled through whatever was under there.

"Junie?" Grace asked, unsure of whether to interrupt her or make her feel more embarrassed by standing up and realizing Grace was there listening to her rant.

Inching forward, Junie knocked her head on the underside of the desk and whipped her head up, rubbing the top of her scalp. Her blue eyes popped open in surprise. "Grace! Hey. Sorry, I'm really not this disorganized usually."

"Are you looking for something?"

"Yeah, I can't find my itinerary for Christmas Eve and Christmas Day. I had everything planned out to a T, from the last shipment the kitchens will be receiving to the product replacements for Tiffany in the spa, to the backup driver for the sleigh ride up the mountain. I'm feeling a little frazzled, that's all." After a quick thought, she held out her hands as if to stop traffic. "But don't worry! This will in no way reflect the quality of your stay here." She added a little wince.

Grace chuckled. "I wasn't worried in the slightest. I only got here last night, and this is already one of my favorite places."

Relief swam across Junie's face. "Oh good. I'm so glad. It's my favorite place in the whole world."

Grace couldn't help smiling around this woman. She was complete vitamin D, and Grace found herself wanting to return the favor somehow. In an instant, she altered her plans to visit the spa. That could be put off for a little while, at least. "Can I help with anything?"

Junie waved her off. "Pfft. No, you're a guest. Go be a guest. Do guestly things. Have you turned in your wish list for your stay here? There's one in every room. See our activities, visit the spa, schedule a sleigh ride—"

"I'm serious," Grace said, ignoring the nagging thought that she really didn't have time for diversions. She had a book to write. Still, she felt bad for Junie and couldn't completely ignore her desire to help. She still had five full days left here. Still plenty of time for writing. Seeing the inner workings of an inn might also get her writing juices going the way meeting Boone had. "I remember you said you were short-staffed. I was going to take a little break anyway. What can I do to help you?"

Junie's shoulders wilted in relief. "Oh, you're an angel. I need to get this shipment taken to the guys out in the barn. You'll have to grab a coat—the only temperature this time of year is two hundred degrees below frostbite."

Grace laughed. "Sure, let me run up to my room and grab it. I'll be right back down."

"With any luck, I'll have found my itinerary by the time you get back," Junie said, ducking back down to peer beneath the desk.

Moving swiftly, Grace made her way up to her room, snatched her coat, swapped out her slippers for the knee-high boots that she zipped over her skinny jeans, and scurried back down. Motivation fueled her. For some reason, she felt more of a thrill helping Junie than she would have had lazing out in the spa. As relaxing as that would have been, she was glad to help the chipper girl.

"Got it!" Junie cried, lifting a paper into the air and waving it the instant Grace reappeared at the base of the stairs.

Grace beamed at her. "Excellent. I knew you would. You know, keeping that kind of thing on a digital planner might make things easier for you."

Junie rolled her eyes with a flare. "You're so right, but I'm the least technological person there is. Blame it on my back-country upbringing." She winked.

"It's all good," Grace said, wrapping her arms around the box. "Is this the one?"

"That's the one. You'll find my cousin in the barn, probably. He's on his break right now and he usually spends his extra time fixing the hay or cleaning stalls or something boring like that. This is the last shipment we'll get before Christmas, so he definitely needs this. Or his horses do."

Grace laughed again and squirmed inside against the little thrill at the excuse to see Boone again. She'd intended on scheduling a sleigh ride with Junie at the desk, but this was ten times better.

Junie held the door open and closed it behind her as Grace stepped out into the sharp, winter air. Peering around the box the best that she could, Grace made her way down the steps, praying she wouldn't hit an unsuspecting patch of ice on the way down, and finally made it to the cleared sidewalk.

Brr. In Scottsdale, the coldest it got was maybe 40 degrees, but this? This was bound to make an ice cube of her if she spent much more time out in it. Grace inwardly thanked her dad for insisting she get the more expensive coat, whose sleeves were even stuffed to block out some of this chill. At least she didn't have far to go.

The elongated, red barn was situated north of the inn, past the parking lot and up the hill just a way. A distinct path had already been trod in the snow to it, and Grace followed that path, making her way to the barn's surrounding stained wooden fencing. A large red sign, positioned across the tall, wooden archway leading into the barnyard, proclaimed *Sleigh Rides*.

Old-fashioned wagon wheels were propped up along the entrance below the tall arched pair of wooden posts. Large, painted candy canes marked each of the posts as well, and Christmas lights strung along the fence. Grace made a mental note to peer out this side of the inn's windows for a view of the barn at night. Clearly, Harper's Inn put on quite a show at night for its guests.

The box in her arms grew heavier with each step. "What is in this thing?" she grumbled out loud, losing her footing and nearly stumbling.

"Easy there," came a gruff voice behind her, its owner's footsteps crunching on the packed snow.

Grace squealed at the unexpected voice. She reared backward and lost her footing. Her boot slipped. She went down to the snowy ground, and the heavy box crashed right on top of her.

"Seriously?" Boone said. Instead of helping her up, he retrieved the box quicker than if it were a lit match nearing a string of gunpowder.

Grace was affronted. "What do you mean, seriously?" she asked. "You act as though I meant to fall." Disappointment thundered down on her like a rockslide. She'd been hoping to talk to him, to tell him she wasn't sure where the necklace had come from, to ask him if he'd heard anything else from the radio.

He'd been brisk and cold with her after their first meeting, but this was downright rude. She was glad he didn't have a free hand to offer her, to help her from the ground. Grace wasn't sure she would have taken it.

"What are you doing carrying packages around? This is important—you have no business interfering around the inn, especially not when shipments won't come up this way again until after Christmas."

Was he lecturing her? Grace brushed the snow from her clothes, wishing she could brush away the cold wetness seeping into her backside just as easily. "Junie asked me to bring this out to you. I told her I would help."

Boone's scowl deepened. "Well, don't. All Junie had to do was call me in. I would have come to get it."

"Fine. Get it yourself then." She was ready to storm away from the neighing horses inside the barn and the sight of a parked sleigh, away from the handsome, infuriating man who was no book hero, thank you very much. At this rate, Grace was ready to make him a villain.

Plot lines exploded in her mind. How could she not have seen this coming before? No wonder she hadn't been able to write him as the love interest earlier. He was no woman's knight in shining armor. This man was all bitter and callous and sour taste. First, he snapped at her over a necklace, and now he was angry at her for helping his cousin?

She was so writing him as a villain.

Grace lifted her chin, sniffed, and scowled at him. Boone's expression softened with the briefest streak of realization as his eyes trapped hers. No longer was his windswept, heartbreaker appearance going to make her swoon, no sir. She'd already fallen at the sound of his voice, and the fall had not boded well. Anyone who was any shade of decent would have set the box aside and helped her up first, or at least shown concern that she'd fallen. Or gratitude for her assistance!

She wasn't about to wait for an apology—not that he would give her one. With a sniff, Grace whipped around and stormed back the way she'd come, beneath the wooden archway and down the snow-trodden path toward the inn.

At this rate, she no longer needed the spa for inspiration. Junie was no longer behind the desk either once Grace made it back inside, and for that, Grace was grateful. She didn't want to replay the horrible interaction to the spunky woman. No way— every ounce of her spiteful thoughts was about to get poured into her novel, into creating the most dastardly, selfish coward her mind could create with the fodder Boone had just handed her.

～

Boone glared after Grace, anger seething in his chest. Every step she took away from him cooled the fire in his chest, though, and he could have sworn he felt the steam emitting from the coals. He hung his head. Once again, his anger had gotten the better of him—and he wasn't even entirely sure what he'd said to her.

He'd reacted, plain and simple. His mind was a thousand places at once and every thought tried skirting away from the sheer irritation he felt just seeing the amount of decorations Junie had insisting on placing at his barn. Anyone coming here would think the candy canes and profusion of lights were his idea.

"The customers need a treat from every angle," Junie had insisted.

Like always, Boone grumbled and went along with it. Because that was his job.

Gripping the box, he trod toward the open barn door, veered through past the bins of hay and feed, and set the package on the wooden table also hosting various jars of remedies for horse's ailments. He was no veterinarian, but he knew a few herbal remedies for helping heal colic and other things horses faced. This was a shipment of oils and herbs for the horses— and its contents weren't exactly cheap. Boone cut across the tape sealing the box together while regret seeped into him.

"Expensive or not," he mumbled, opening the box, "I still shouldn't have snapped at her."

Uncertainty stole over him one layer at a time. This wasn't the first time he'd snapped at an unsuspecting recipient. Boone had never been short-tempered before, but it seemed that more and more, anger was becoming his default setting. His recent conversation with Junie about the radio attempting to match him with Grace didn't help.

Why anger, though? What about him had changed? He'd only done his best to keep to himself. To deal with Amy's passing. He was gentle and careful with the horses and the children at the inn. But he'd gone and snapped at Grace not once, but twice. First, over the necklace, and now this. She must think he was a total bear.

He shook his head at that thought. What did he care what she or any woman thought of him?

He didn't care. He couldn't. Especially not her.

_____

7

"Oh yeah," Grace said, her fingers flying over the keys. She was situated on the armchair in the inn's living room. With the fire crackling, and the inn's designated "Social Hour" passed, she essentially had the room to herself. Her feet were propped on the footstool, the lights beamed and twinkled in unison on the elaborate Christmas tree beside her, and she was completely in the zone.

Demon Boone had dark hair, a pointed nose, and a sinister laugh which he directed at anyone foolish enough to not understand his impressive wit and dastardly evil schemes. Grace decided she would fill in his name later once she found a decent replacement. But for now, she reveled in calling him Demon Boone.

He stormed his snowy castle, spewing expletives and evil curses at servants and condemning the heroic tree-born hero with pointed ears and an affinity for trouble. This was going to be good. So good. So much better than her first manuscript—The One That Got Away, she was starting to call it.

No rejections would come to this one, no sirree. She could feel it with every word that clacked out from her fingertips and filled the white page on her screen. Her word count climbed higher and higher, ticking up like a victory banner on its way to fifty thousand words.

"Hey, there, Grace," Junie said, peeking in.

Grace concentrated, not wanting to let go of the last threads of delicious banter her characters were engaging in. Finally at a stopping point, she peered up. Junie smirked from the doorway. Instead of the sweater and jeans she'd worn earlier, she was in gray pajamas with pink snowflakes on them, and her long brown hair hung past her shoulders instead of in their usual braids. The combination made her appear much older than she usually did. It made Grace wonder how old she really was.

"Hi, Junie. How did the rest of your day go?"

She padded farther in on her stocking feet and nestled on the chair across from Grace. "Oh, great. So great. Just trying to keep things going the best I can, you know? What about you? I assume things went okay taking the box out."

"Not exactly," Grace said. "I mean, I got it out to him all right, but—"

"Let me guess. He was less than friendly."

"Something like that." Grace smiled to lessen her irritation.

"Don't take it personally," Junie said, her knees bouncing as if she had excess energy. "We're working on his customer service. It's just that Boone's had things a little rough. Not saying there's an excuse for his behavior, and if I were anyone else, I would have fired him by now. But he's family."

"I get that," Grace said, not wanting to let her desire to know more about him take over. She was aching—dying—to ask what kind of rough things Boone was dealing with to make him so snappish. She had to admit, she wasn't always a ray of sunshine, especially not when things were going wrong. Maybe she'd just caught him at a bad time.

Even still, she wasn't going to go easy on him. He was a villain, and he was going to stay that way.

"I can't tell you how awesome it was for you to offer to help me."

Grace was happy for the different topic. "It was no problem at all. You helped me too, though you don't realize it."

Junie's eyes lit up. "Really? I'm so glad! Is that what you're working on?"

"It's a book. I'm—"

Grace's phone rang. Though the sound was on silent, the screen blared in the dimly lit room.

Junie rose hastily from her seat. "I'll let you get that. It was good talking to you today, Grace. Have a good night."

"Thanks, Junie. You too." Mom's goofy grin filled Grace's screen. With a smile, she swiped to answer, eager to give her an update on her book. Because this was why she was here. Not men. Books.

"Hey, Mom."

"Hey, Gracie girl," Mom said. "I'm not calling too late, am I? I know you're an hour off from us."

Tiredness prickled at Grace's eyes as if her fatigue sensed its cue to make an appearance. Grace closed her laptop and readjusted her feet so she could cocoon herself on the comfortable armchair. "Not too late. I'm in the most amazing room here. It's like a fairy tale. You'd love this place."

"That's so great, honey. And how's the writing?"

Exuberance filled Grace's tone. "Amazing. This book is practically writing itself."

"Excellent! So you're almost done with it?"

Grace heard an edge to Mom's voice that she didn't have a moment before. Gripping her laptop with her free hand, she rested her feet on the floor. "Why do you say it like that?"

"Oh, nothing sweetie. Nothing at all. It's just that..."

Dad's voice was heard in the background. Mom shushed him. "She needs to know this, Robert. We have to at least tell her."

Grace's attention pricked. She sat up a little straighter. "You have to at least tell me what?" Had something happened to her sister? Was everyone okay?

Mom made a stifling noise between clicking her tongue and a cough. "I wasn't sure whether I should say anything or not, Gracie. It's just that—well, I mean, if your book is practically done and writing itself, there's nothing saying you can't finish it say, tomorrow, right? Or on the plane even."

"Mom," Grace said with a warning tone. "Don't do this to me. I'm having a great time here." At least, as long as she avoided the grumpy, grouchy-pants cowboy.

"I know, and I'm so glad. That's all we wanted for you. It's just that—"

"What, Mom?" Grace hoped this wasn't about the guy Uncle Mike was bringing home.

"We just heard from Stephanie. Sounds like Miles is surprising her with a trip home for Christmas as his gift to her this year."

Grace bolted upright in the chair, nearly knocking her laptop off her lap. "What?"

"Yes! Honey, they're driving home, and they'll be bringing that sweet baby so you can finally meet your niece!"

Excitement fought with disappointment inside of her. Her sister was coming to Arizona for Christmas! She hadn't seen Stephanie in almost two years, and though they chatted online every few days, that still wasn't the same as heading out for custard at their favorite parlor or window shopping at the mall while they talked and caught one another up on all the little things they'd missed in each other's lives. Stephanie was a few years older than Grace's twenty-two, and Grace had always looked up to her big sister.

Better still, Grace would finally get to squish baby Molly's cheeks and cuddle her like she'd wanted to every time she saw a picture of their adorable, chubby, bright-eyed baby. She'd wanted to hold the baby since the pictures first started rolling in.

Stephanie's husband had gotten a job in Florida just after they'd gotten married. When Molly was born six months ago, Mom had flown out to help and had stayed for two weeks. Grace had wanted to go, but hadn't been able to manage it.

"How long are they staying?" Grace asked.

"Until the day after Christmas. Gracie, I know the idea was for you to stay during your time off work, but you can get your money refunded, right? I would so love to be with both of my girls at Christmas. I haven't had the two of you home together in so long."

Grace rubbed her forehead, fighting the conflict inside of her.

Mom went on. "Not to mention Uncle Mike bringing that guy home to meet you. I just—" Dad said something else in the background, but Mom ignored him. Grace wished she would listen to whatever Dad was saying. She loved Mom and had told her before to stop setting her up on awkward, unwanted dates. Uncle Mike wasn't one to intrude in Grace's love life, but her mother sure was.

"Mom," Grace began, trying to derail this thought train. "What is it you're wanting me to do?" She was already here. This trip was her parents' gift to her; they had already spent money on the flight and on her room and she still hadn't finished her book. She didn't know what to do. Surely, as they grew older, getting together as a family would become harder and harder. Was this the start of that phase of life?

"I know the plan was for you to stay during your time off

work," Mom said, "but honey, is there any way you can come home a few days early? You can work on your book here! It would mean so much to me." Dad muttered something again, and Grace wished she knew what he'd said. Did he think Mom was being unreasonable?

"It's our Stephie!" Mom said, continuing her verbal crusade. "Plus, I think Uncle Mike might really be bugged if he's gone through all the trouble of inviting this guy along to meet you and you're not even here."

"Mom," Grace said, realizing a frustrated whine had seeped through. "Coming here was your Christmas present to me. It's like you're taking it away."

"Don't you want to see Stephanie?"

"Of course I do!" But she refused to let Mom make this about some random guy Grace had no interest in meeting.

"Mike showed me pictures. Terry really is handsome, and you never know what can happen. But you'll certainly never know if you're not here. I know how you and your sister used to like to check out the guys. You never know what might happen with Stephanie here for you to talk to!"

Grace bristled. The guilt trip where Stephanie was concerned was probably justified, but adding the blind date into the argument wasn't Mom's greatest tactic. Boone's coldness toward her outside the barn earlier replayed in solemn, grisly fashion. Grace's girlish hopes for something with him were obviously misplaced, as would be any hopes Mom had of something sparking between her and this blind date guy.

"I'm here to work on my novel, Mother. You guys already paid for the room and my plane tickets. I would dearly love to see Stephanie and hold that baby of hers, but I feel like I'm stuck. I still have four more days here. I'm not cutting my trip short just so I can meet a guy." Another rejection. That was all it would be. She'd had plenty of those, from agents and men alike. Boone's actions earlier stung that much harder at the thought.

She didn't need Mom's matchmaking attempts. How could Mom do this to her? She knew the way stories thrived inside of Grace, begging to be put to paper. What good was writing a story if no one ever read them? Grace wanted to hit it big. She loved getting immersed in a story and talking to friends about their latest reads. She wanted *her* books to be talked about. To be raved over.

Sure, she was excited with her progress, but that didn't mean the book was ready. And it certainly didn't mean that Grace was ready to leave.

"I understand if you want to stay," Mom said. "But Stephanie will be so disappointed to come all this way and not see you. If that wasn't the case, of course I'd want you to stay so you could work on your book."

Grace exhaled.

"The choice is up to you, sweetie," Mom finally said, with that cunning lining she occasionally applied for instances such as this.

Guilt answered the call and began to build up inside of her. She hated this. How could she stay here now, knowing she would be letting Mom down if she stayed? Knowing that Stephanie and her sweet baby would be home—home!—and Grace wasn't there?

There was still so much to do here. So much to explore. She hadn't tried the Chef's Tasting Menu, which was going to be offered the following evening. She so craved the restorative massage she'd read all about. Not to mention the sleigh rides and the surrounding forest that she'd meant to include as part of her fantasy world.

Blocks settled in her brain, ramming against the inspiration and creativity that had flowed so freely minutes before. Grace grasped for them, wanting to reawaken the muse, but it burrowed as if nestling in for some serious hibernation.

That alone was enough to make her want to cry.

How could she call it back now? Conscience had settled in, taking the muse's place. She wanted to stick to her resolve, to continue with the plans she had already concocted before even coming here. But her determination to stay through Christmas and a few days beyond to get all her words in melted, shriveling like a snowman too close to the fire.

Grace rolled her eyes. Every one of her arguments skittered. She wanted to hang up. To tell her mom she was a grown woman and could make her own decisions. But the words wouldn't come. And really, what did writing a book matter when seeing her sister was so much more important?

"Okay," Grace heard herself say.

"Really?" Mom's reply was nearly a shriek. Dad muttered something again and Mom answered him, "She said she's coming home, Robert. No—this was her idea, not mine!"

Grace could picture her parents in their usual argument. Any other time it would have made her smile, but the gloom that sometimes came with doing the right thing instead of sticking with what you personally wanted was settling in fast.

She forced a smile. This was the right thing to do. There would still be time to finish her book, but she would be devastated if she had the chance to see her sister and niece and hadn't taken it.

"Excellent, sweetie," Mom said. "You won't regret this, and I promise, Dad and I will make it up to you. We'll take a drive up to Jackson Hole or the Grand Canyon this summer or something. This will be so great! Both my girls home for Christmas! I'll see you soon, right? No later than Christmas Eve?"

"Sure," she answered heartlessly, staring around at the inn. What was the point of coming here? She never should have come. All the magic this place had offered her since the moment she'd arrived vanished.

With forlorn steps, Grace trudged up to her room. She didn't want to go back home. Breathing so much open air, having the freedom to rove without roasting in the blazing heat, interacting with people in person instead of angry and frustrated customers on the other end of the line who seemed to think that because she worked for the company she was responsible for their dissatisfaction.

Grace hadn't even realized it until now, but the longer she was here, she less she wanted to leave. She wanted a different life. One where she could be outside, where she could write and breathe.

But she lived in Arizona. That was where her apartment was, where her job was, where her family was. Her mom was right—Stephanie was coming. Grace needed to get home. Why didn't the thought make her feel any better about it?

After a long shower—and a good long cry in the hot water where no one else would hear—Grace decided something. She would reschedule her flight and go home early. She would see her sister and her cute baby, appease her mom, *and* finish her book before Christmas break ended.

But if she was leaving, she intended on getting at least one sleigh ride. She needed some one-on-one time with the snowy woods around here, too. Even if she didn't get the actual writing done, she was gathering data that could be used later.

And yes, she fully realized this meant also having some alone time with the inn's sexy, surly sleigh driver.

8

Boone stood in the barn's opening for several moments. He'd just gotten off the phone with Troy, who had taken the day off to be with his father in the hospital. His dad, Rick, had a broken tibia and needed to have his hip replaced as a result of the fall. Boone had sent his apologies and condolences and assured Troy he already had someone lined up to fill in for his dad over Christmas Eve and Christmas Day.

"So great, man," Troy had said. "Thank you. I can't tell you what it means to me, and that you and Junie sent food for my mom. She's just dealing with so much, you know?"

"I think the time of year adds unnecessary stress," Boone had said.

Troy only laughed at that and then assured Boone he would be there first thing in the morning. Boone thanked him and hung up. And though he'd given Troy the reassurance that everything was fine, and he was happy to take on Troy's scheduled rides for the day, the stress of adding two more jaunts that afternoon tightened everything inside of him like a ratchet strap.

"Hey, hey, Boone!" Junie's voice reached him before he saw her climbing up the walk in his direction. She was always so loud, so goofy, so not-caring about what others thought of her. He had to admit, she added a flare to the inn that guests loved. But did she have to shout his name?

"Hey, cuz," she said again, slightly breathless as she stepped closer. Pink tinged her freckled cheeks, and her smile showcased a single crooked tooth in the front.

"I'm standing right here," he said. "You don't have to shout at me."

"Someone's in a good mood," she said sarcastically, holding out the papers in her hand.

He groaned. "You're kidding, right?"

"What?"

He snatched the proffered papers and looked them over. Sure enough, the guests had filled out wish lists. These people were also signed up to attend the Christmas Eve bonfire. Why in the heck did they want another sleigh ride if they were already going on one?

"I just talked to Troy, and I'm taking his clients today," Boone said with a growl.

"Perfect!"

"Does nothing faze you?"

"I don't see what the problem is. You work here."

"The horses can only handle so much," he said. He could only handle so much was what he should have said. "Not to mention the sleigh maintenance that might pop up. And yet you're giving me more?"

Junie folded her arms. The smile streaked away from her cheeks. "Like it or not, it's Christmas, and people are depending on us." She jabbed a finger between them. "Not to mention there's a leak in the kitchen roof that I need you to look at when you get back."

"Of course there is," Boone said. "You mean Mason can't fix it?"

Her eyes thinned to slits. "Don't be mean. You were never mean, Boone."

A small amount of shame struck him. The comment was low —he was just tired of being the only one expected to fix anything around here. Maybe they should hire a maintenance guy, but the inn didn't bring in that much revenue. Or so Junie claimed.

"Not everyone's talents lie in repairs," Junie went on. "You grew up doing that kind of thing around here with your dad, so you know exactly what to do. Besides, Mason is busy prepping the pastries for Christmas morning, and that's a real art."

Boone snorted.

She looked as if she was ready to stab him. But this was sweet, spunky Junie. He always got under her skin, and then she always got over it.

"You know, you'd think all this extra work would help you get over yourself," she said.

"Get over myself?"

"You're so stuck in the past, Boone, you can't even see what people are doing around you."

"Not again. We're not doing this again."

"Oh, that's right, you're too busy feeling sorry for yourself. Well, news flash, dear cousin of mine, you aren't the only person in existence! The radio knows it and I know it. Time for you to get a clue."

Junie stormed off and left him by himself before he could craft any kind of reply. He stood there, staring at the white terrain beneath the sky's piercing blue, and watched her stalk away.

That seemed to happen a lot lately, especially when he was interacting with women. Troy and his father never got angry at him. The guys were chill and easygoing, but for some reason, his interactions with women were like sandpaper against skin.

Shaking his head, Boone turned back to finish what he'd come here to do. He shoveled the pitchfork hard into the pile of straw and distributed it along the newly cleaned corrals in the barn, inhaling the scent of the straw. He was completely fuming by the time he finished, and not just over the amount of extra work she'd thrust at him. Junie had no right to go and make assumptions about his state of mental health or his need for relationships.

Was he closed off? Yes. By choice. By preference. That didn't mean he was *selfish*. He thought, of all people, his cousin would understand that.

Junie was one of the few people who understood just how crushing losing his wife had been. She'd been there the night he'd finally cried, letting his emotions dominate. He'd kept them in for so long that they started to turn to stone in his chest and rattled around inside of him with every step he took. They grew heavier and heavier, and every night alone at the cottage he shoved them deeper inside of himself, to the darkest parts he rarely let surface.

Junie thought the radio was being some kind of matchmaker. She'd never been married; she was probably willing to accept that explanation and had probably had it confirmed by her mom. But Boone couldn't allow another woman into his life. He'd already learned too late what a fool he was for caring so much. Why give his heart away to someone else who had the power to break it all over again?

No, thank you.

Behind him, a horse chuffed and the sound of someone walking across the scattered hay met Boone's ears. He thought it might have been Hazelnut, but he wasn't sure. When he turned to see, he wished he hadn't. Grace Eastland dusted her gloved hands and treaded warily through the barn, as though it was her first time setting foot in one. Her golden hair hung in waves beneath a white beanie that matched her gloves, and a timid smile added light to the caution in her eyes.

They weren't striking. They weren't lovely. She wasn't beautiful. She didn't make his heart pick up speed or split cracks into the wall he'd so carefully placed to guard himself from ever giving it away again.

Yet, every one of those arguments drifted like a leaf in the wind. Boone was well aware that the last time they'd spoken he hadn't exactly been on his best behavior. What was she doing here now?

His irritation triggered again, considering the way Junie just left. His cousin didn't have something to do with this, with Grace waltzing in here, did she? He should never have told Junie both he and Grace had heard the blasted radio play.

"Hey, there," Grace said. Even the sweet tone of her voice plucked at one of the strings knotting in his chest, threatening to unravel him. He knew he should apologize for practically biting her head off. He'd thought over the instance multiple times since it had happened. Slipping and falling wasn't her fault. He'd just been on edge.

He grunted and thrust the pitchfork into the straw again. He had to remember, she was a guest. He could be civil to guests. But being civil to her seemed like a promise of something more than just cordiality. Why did a smile and a kind word feel like he was letting down a link on the chain to the drawbridge guarding his heart?

"Can I help you with something?" he asked.

"My plans have changed, and it looks like I won't be able to stay through Christmas after all. I'm headed home tomorrow. I know I'm not on your schedule or anything—and I couldn't find the other driver to ask." She winced at this. "So anyway, it's just you left here. I know it's probably too much, but do you mind squeezing in one more ride tonight before I have to leave? With me? I mean, *for* me?"

He shouldn't care about her plans. He shouldn't ask more about her. But the pull to find out more was too strong to deny. "What changed?"

"It's my mom," she said with a sigh. "She's pretty insistent I go home. There's a guy coming for Christmas to meet me, I guess. And my sister living across the country is coming home last minute. I haven't met her new baby yet, and this might be my only chance for a while."

The idea of her with someone else twisted inside of him, though he couldn't figure out why. This was good. She should go home. She should be with someone else.

He sought for an excuse not to take her. "I have two rides scheduled for today. Hazelnut will be pretty tuckered out by then." Not to mention, Hazelnut wasn't the inn's horse like some of the others. She belonged to Boone and she was his ride home, since Junie didn't like Boone taking the snowmobile back and forth to work. He didn't want to wear too much on the mare, and she was his favorite to take on sleigh rides because she was so reliable.

"I have to leave at five a.m. tomorrow if I want to make this flight I just rescheduled," she said. "I know I'm asking a lot, but please? We won't have to go far. I don't want to go home without taking in as much of the scenery here as I can. The scenery is why I came in the first place." She added a hopeless smile to the statement, as though leaving wasn't what she wanted at all.

Boone rubbed his chin. The bit about Hazelnut was a stretch, if he were being honest. The horse would be fine with one more ride. He could practically hear Junie screaming at him from her position as his boss, rather than just his cousin. They needed to maintain a good reputation with their customers at the inn, and many people traveled here just for the scenery and the sleigh rides.

Tomorrow was Christmas Eve. He usually took Christmas Eve and Christmas Day off, so even if Grace were staying, he wouldn't be around to drive her the next day as it was. Hazelnut would be up for a jaunt before taking Boone back to his cottage, to hide away, to lose himself in solitude while he painstakingly waited for Christmas to get itself over with.

"All right," Boone said, splitting like a baked potato. "I can make an exception for you. Hazelnut should have one more ride in her."

Grace's blue eyes lit up. Her delight was like a sunrise. "Thank you! What time should I plan on?"

He glanced at the clock on his phone. "I should be getting back with the last party around five. Then, since it's just the two of us, I've got to get her harnessed back up again, to the smaller rig this time." He gestured past the larger, cherry red sleigh with three rows for passengers, to the smaller, white single seater. He also calculated the time it would take for him to grab a bite to eat. "So how does six o'clock sound?"

Her smile stretched. She had amazing teeth and immaculate skin. Amy had always struggled with breakouts, but that didn't seem to be something this woman would ever have to battle.

Ugh. Where did that thought come from? Too late, he realized she'd already spoken. "Sorry?" he said.

Her smile slipped. She looked him over as if questioning his sanity. "I said that will be great," she said.

He gave an abrupt nod. "Okay then."

"And Boone?"

He prepared to turn away from her but paused in the act. She took a tentative step closer. Just one step. "Thank you. I know you don't like me much, but this means a lot to me." She pressed her lips into a contrite but grateful expression and whirled away from him before he could say anything else.

Breathing became a foreign concept. She thought he didn't like her much? He had done his best to give that impression, he supposed. Why, then, did he suddenly want to change her opinion? It shouldn't matter what he thought of her. After their ride, he would never be seeing this woman again.

That was right. He'd never see her again. He was being stupid. She was a guest, nothing more.

The least he could do was be civil. Not for Junie, but because for some reason, the fact that Grace called him out on his behavior in such a non-confrontational way made him want to change it. To let her know he wasn't all prickles.

That settled it. During their ride, he would apologize. He would be kind to her and show her he was a decent human being.

Grace cursed herself the entire way back to the inn and up to her room. "I know you don't like me, but thank you?" she muttered, wanting to shake herself. What did she say that for?

He would be a grump during their entire sleigh ride. She would just have to ignore him, that was all. He couldn't snap at her if she didn't say anything to him, right? She was going there to write. She would drink in the sights and scribble every thought that came to her. Less interruptions would be all the better.

Still, she buzzed with emotion and anticipation. The same urge that came over her whenever a new idea struck took over in spite of the block she'd felt since Mom's phone call, and since calling Stephanie shortly afterward. She'd called her sister and mentioned she would be flying in the next day. Stephanie hadn't seemed to know Grace was even away from home, which meant Mom had already assumed Grace would be coming back before she'd called to twist Grace's arm into it. Which had blocked Grace's muse with her frustration even more. Yes, she definitely had to write this while the sensations were fresh and feelable.

She plopped on the floral armchair, pen in hand, and submersed herself in her thoughts. Everything she'd written about Demon Boone had been stellar. He was cruel and cunning. He killed his enemies and even his own soldiers without a thought and inflicted torture with all the delight and craftiness of a maimed soul. Grace couldn't wait to have her heroine strike him down with unforeseen magic. Multiple times.

But something about this latest interaction with Boone had been different than his brusque, snappish manner. He'd shown remorse—if not verbally, then in his eyes. Their expression had reached through her. Something about him had been so different in the barn.

An image of Boone floated forward in her mind. His dark, sultry eyes, his brooding, handsome features, his closed-off reticence and the way his mere proximity made her come alive—in spite of herself. So he was attractive. So what? The rest of him was decidedly *not*.

Writing had always been therapeutic for her, and she shifted her focus, smoothing a hand over her notebook's empty page. She could craft him, she supposed, and assign her fictional love interest with some of Boone's traits, the way she'd done with her villain momentarily named Demon Boone.

But this was different. Whatever the emotions raging inside of her were, they were raw and real, and writing always helped her sort out her thoughts. The truth was, Boone had a glance that made her come apart at the seams and be instantly stitched together all over again. He had such a strong effect on her, one she couldn't justify, considering how closed-off and downright rude he was.

I shouldn't be feeling this way, she wrote. *Boone is all cactus, letting me know the minute I get too close I'll get pricked. He's a mirage in the desert, seeming to be one thing but turning out to be something else entirely the closer I get.*

But every time he looks at me, it's like the world stops spinning. Everyone and everything else in the room disappears. He's all I see, and I'm not sure if it's because of me or because some otherworldly force is attempting to push us together.

I don't know what haunts him. Sometimes he's courteous, but it seems like he's trying so hard to keep everyone around him at arm's length. I'm not even sure what I'm hoping for with him because, in all truth, wanting more with him at all makes no sense, but he's awoken something in my heart that I didn't know I could feel. I think that's what makes his standoffish behavior so confusing. It must only be one-sided. I must be the only one feeling this way, because he clearly has no interest in me.

I've never believed in fate or magic, though I write about both, but a man like Boone makes me believe both concepts are not only plausible, but possible. We've shared only a few words, and not always nice ones at that.

I think I just want this...whatever it is between us...to mean something. When he looks at me, it's like more than our gazes connect. It's an unspoken invitation, and all I want is to be wherever he is. I guess I just want a reason for the mere sight of him to be such a bulldozer to my entire existence.

I want to believe fate does exist and we're meant to be.

But fate doesn't exist.

I know rejection all too well. Boone Harper is just a rejection waiting to happen.

Grace exhaled once her soul finished purging itself through her pen. She couldn't explain these feelings. She couldn't justify them. But somehow, the admission just felt *right*.

"It's for my book," she told herself. She was here at Harper's Inn for a reason. Boone was the research she needed to create a dreamy love interest readers would swoon over. Nothing more. She would go on this sleigh ride, and then she would go home and forget all about him.

Her phone chirped. She glanced at the clock, and her pulse hiccupped in response. It was nearly time.

Tension injected into her veins. Grace slammed her notebook closed and stuffed it into her bright blue, slouchy, crocheted bag along with a few pens, a snack, and her phone. She collected her gloves, stuffed her beanie over her long, wavy blonde hair, and headed outside.

It was time to go dashing through the snow.

10

D usk was approaching. The sky had turned a listless shade of palest blue, the kind of blue getting ready to pack it in for the night and settle into something deeper and more restful. Grace's breath seeped out from her mouth like smoke in a way she was coming to love. How adventurous was this, to see her own breath? She plodded through the snow, following the same path she'd taken to the barn before, only this time her hands were free of the cumbersome box.

To her delight, the lights she'd noticed strung along the fence and lining the edges of the barn's roof were now lit, as were the candy canes marking the sides of the archway. With the barn illuminated as it was, it stood like a cheerful beacon on the mountainside. She couldn't wait to see it in total darkness.

Grace tucked her chin into the top of her zipped-up coat and allowed her gaze to roam. She would never forget Harper's Inn and the way just standing here, alone, beneath the sweeping sky and surrounded by trees and everything winter made her feel special, like she was blessed to be here and experience this for herself. No number of pictures, beautiful as they were, could capture the *feeling* of standing beneath a sky like this, of imitating the crisp, fresh smell of the cold air and the way it filled her lungs.

The sound of jingling bells pulled her attention toward the barn. Boone walked alongside the speckled gray horse who lifted its hooves elegantly over the white ground. Harnessed to the single, white sleigh Grace had noticed in the barn the day before, the horse pulled the sleigh at a slow pace. Grace quickened her own, climbing up the rise to meet Boone.

A thick hat covered his head and ears, though tufts of dark hair spoked from the line of his hat across his forehead. His eyes had a hint of light that wasn't usually there, and he smiled—smiled!—at her.

"Evening, Grace," he said, tipping his head in her direction. The horse beside him stopped, as did the jingle bells on its harness. "How was your afternoon?"

Grace wasn't sure how to handle this friendly version of him. Her mouth hung open and she had to remind herself to close it. "Fine," she said abruptly, gripping the strap of her bag.

He spoke softly to the mare, patting his gloved hand along her neck, and circled around to the side of the sleigh. To her surprise, the sleigh was a single model, without even a driver's seat. He would be driving the sleigh...beside her?

"I hope this one is okay. The other one needed some repairs."

Boone climbed up onto the sleigh and settled in, gathering the reins in both hands. The horse shuffled the snow with her hooves. Feeling suddenly shy, Grace hesitated at the prospect of sharing the cramped bench with him. She realized she still hadn't responded to his remark. Reins in one hand, he rested a glove on the front and looked at her.

"Are you coming?" he asked.

She chewed her lip and then climbed onto the sleigh's metal frame. Cold bit through her thin gloves. She took the flannel-lined bench beside him, but the fabric was cold there too. Everything was cold—except for the flames blushing in her cheeks. Could he see? Was she turning red?

"Here," Boone said, shaking out a woolen blanket similar to the one covering his lap. The fabric was just large enough to place over her legs and tuck in around her. Inadvertently, she bumped an elbow against his arm. "Sorry," she mumbled. Boone cleared his throat and kept his gaze facing forward while she settled herself and placed her bag at her feet.

They sat side by side long enough without moving that Grace began to wonder if everything was okay. She turned slightly to ask when Boone faced her at the same time. Their knees touched, sending flurries into her stomach.

Boone cleared his throat and mumbled something.

"What was that?" she said kindly.

He gripped the reins, staring at his hands, and then seemed to decide on something. He nodded as if agreeing with himself and then turned to her. "Before we head out, I owe you an apology."

She dipped her head. "No, it's okay," she began, but he continued.

"Please, let me say this. I haven't behaved as I should have. I know you were only helping Junie out that day, the day you brought my supplies out and then slipped on the snow. I was an idiot. I should have helped you up—I should never have barked at you the way I did. It's just, I know there's no excuse. But I'm sorry."

Her cheeks blazed under his direct gaze and the sincerity in his words. She searched his brown eyes, eager for any hint that he might be insincere, but she found nothing but the connection she'd always felt every time their eyes met.

"Thank you," she said. "I appreciate that."

He pressed his lips together and inclined his head at her.

Grace continued to examine him even as he turned his attention toward the horse. She could tell the effect the blanket had at keeping warmth over her lower half. The left side of her body lit up at Boone's proximity, more so since his heartfelt apology. There wasn't much space to scoot away from him in this smaller, more intimate model.

"I think we'll make my usual trek through the woods, down to the skating pond, and then take the scenic route back," he said. "How does that sound?"

"Isn't it all a scenic route?"

This gave him only a moment's pause. To her surprise, the corner of his mouth quirked up in a halfway grin. "I guess it is. Are you ready?"

She glanced toward her feet, ensuring her blue, crocheted bag was slouched where she'd placed it. Grace was reminded of the mesh bags provided on roller coasters for people to tuck their personal belongings in during a wild ride. This wouldn't be nearly as high speed as anything like that.

"Ready," she said, smiling at him.

Again, he returned the smile, catching her completely off-balance. His glance lingered longer than was customary, and she wondered if he wanted to say something. Pressing his lips into a thin line, he gave a small smirk and glanced away.

Grace swallowed, unsure of what had changed between them since she'd spoken with him earlier. No snide remarks. No snappish comments. Was it because she was a paid customer now? Sleigh rides weren't complimentary during her stay; she'd put in her deposit at the front desk before coming out here.

That had to be it.

Boone gripped the reins and clicked his teeth, calling out with a grunt that the horse responded to.

They rode in silence for a few minutes while Grace adjusted to the feel of the cold air brushing against her bare cheeks. Her chest and arms were completely warm, however, and for that she was grateful. She had fully intended on keeping quiet for the entire duration of their ride, but she couldn't help the small exclamations that kept spilling from her lips.

"Exquisite," she said, taking in the sight of a stray deer with white spots along its back, pausing to glance over at them as they passed. "How often do you see things like that?"

The question was meant to be rhetorical, but Boone replied. "A lot, actually. I see all kinds of wildlife here. The other night I had a raccoon scratching at my door."

"You're kidding."

There was that sideways grin again. "Nope. I see a lot of deer, squirrels, no bears yet, thankfully, but then, with the movement at the inn and the cars coming and going, they tend to keep their distance."

Grace shuddered. Bears. That was definitely not something she wanted to come face to face with. "You must ferry a lot of people around here."

"I do. I take a few batches of guests out every single day."

The snow stole her attention for a moment while she searched for something to say. "So this is what you do here at Harper's Inn? You're the sleigh driver."

"I help with maintenance around the inn and offer horse-drawn sleigh rides. It's one thing to ride in a car on a road through the mountains, but it's completely different riding out *in* the scenery. Horses offer a slower pace, and the sleigh provides a more romantic setting."

The shift to this topic surprised her. "Every person who comes here can't possibly be after a romantic excursion."

He didn't so much as crack a smile. "Not every person, but a lot of people are. Besides, romance doesn't always apply to love. It used to mean like, mystery and excitement, something set apart from regular life. That's how I meant it."

As if her heart needed another reason to pat a little faster. His comment resonated. Here was a man with an affinity for words. Words were Grace's everything, and not only did he know an older context for something, but he used it in a way that completely defined what he was describing for her at the same time.

The snow blanketing the mountainside, climbing up the trees so their branches skirted its surface, was smooth and unblemished. It didn't have so much as a footprint and was just waiting to be explored. Talk about romantic.

"That's completely *romantic* that you knew that," Grace said.

He slid his gaze to her. "I aim to impress."

"Then you hit the bullseye."

The smallest trace of delight flashed in his eyes, and his stony expression cracked just enough that she caught a glimpse of his dimple. Small victories.

"How many sleigh rides do you end up offering a day?"

"Depends on the day," he said as the horse trotted before them, jingling all the way. Strips of dark leather holding shining silver bells chimed with every step the gray horse took. "And the number of guests. Most of the time it's about three rides a day. I'm doing this one since it's so close to Christmas. Junie and her mom agree the sleigh rides add an ambience to the inn that other places don't have."

"What do you do in the summertime, when there's no snow?"

"Hayrides," he said. "Or horseback riding. You think it's beautiful now, you should see this place during the summer. Everything is so green and lush. There's a small pond that way" —he pointed with his gloved hand— "that beavers build little dams in every year. And the wildflowers in the meadow are pretty incredible."

"That sounds amazing, but I'm not sure anything compares

to this." Grace glanced up at the tops of the trees making their steep climb to the gray-blue sky. He was right; driving past a mountain in a car was one thing. But at the horse's slower speeds, with the sound of the runners sliding on the snow and the horse's jingling movements, the frigid air didn't seem quite so cold.

Or maybe it was just sitting so close to Boone.

11

"Winter is my favorite too." His admission held a trace of reluctance. Grace wondered if the same elephant accompanying her through this journey was also apparent to him. She hadn't forgotten his rudeness toward her earlier. Was that why he was being so kind now?

She considered asking about the necklace he'd yanked from her hand, about whether the radio had played again or where he'd managed to stash it when he stormed off with it, but they'd reached a kind of camaraderie that she didn't want to spoil.

"Do you ever take big crowds?" she asked, remembering the larger sleigh she'd seen in the barn.

"Sometimes I take just a single couple out," he said. "Depends on the request. You can't believe the number of marriage proposals I overhear."

Grace's laugh was belly deep and genuine and echoed off the mountainside. "I'm sure you do."

Boone cracked another timid smile but fought it down again. Why did he do that? What made him so hesitant to open up to her?

The cold air kissed her bare skin. She shivered. This

reminded her of reading *Little House on the Prairie,* and how they bundled up and used warm potatoes in their pockets to keep their hands warm while riding on a sleigh through the woods. Imagine traveling by horse-drawn sleigh as your only means of transportation.

"I worried about spending money on snow gear like hats and beanies before I left, but now I'm glad I did."

"Where are you from that it doesn't get cold enough for beanies and gloves?" he asked.

"Scottsdale, Arizona."

Boone grunted in displeasure. "Too hot for my blood," he said.

Grace quirked a brow. "Have you ever been there?"

"Yes. I visited my brother during a real estate scheme he tried talking me into." He directed a scowl toward the horse's backside as if he didn't like the memory of it.

"Let me guess, you didn't pursue the scheme."

Boone angled his head. His face lightened as if at some inward joke. "There may be money in real estate, but I couldn't take care of my horses if I was busy flipping houses or attending auctions."

Grace smiled. This time he let his gaze linger long enough to take in her appearance. His direct glance made her blood still. She hadn't meant to draw attention to her appearance. The hat had only been a topic of conversation. Yet, he glanced at her, eyes roving over her face with a calculating quality. She swallowed a lump in her throat. Did he like what he saw? Did he feel the same pull she felt toward him?

"What?" she asked.

"That's a Santa Claus hat," he said after a few moments, turning his attention back to the horse.

She clapped her hand over her soft, slouchy beanie. "It's not red."

"Doesn't have to be."

She blew warm air through her thin gloves. "You talk about him like you still believe in him," she said. He'd mentioned as much in the inn, but she wasn't sure he was being serious.

"I never stopped believing," he said. "Journey told me not to."

The dry joke descended slowly. Grace laughed when it landed. "That is one of the best songs."

He darted another glance in her direction, his lips tweaking just enough to portray amusement. Delight danced in his eyes. "Agreed."

Feeling bolstered by the ease of their conversation, Grace sat a little straighter. He was fighting smiles. That was progress too. "Okay, then. We both like words and their definitions. We both like Journey."

"But I can't get around all that heat down in Arizona," he said.

"Sometimes I can't either," she admitted. "I've always wanted to come to a place like this. To see snow like this." She gestured to the loveliness around her. Fading sunlight played on the snow. The clear sky peeked through gaps in the trees. A contended sigh escaped her lips.

"Is that what brought you here?" he asked.

"Sort of. I'm here on a research trip."

His brows rose. "West Hills, Montana, is in the middle of nowhere. What can you possibly have to research around here?"

"The middle of nowhere," she said with a chuckle.

Speaking of which, this was as good a time as any to pull out her notebook. After their chuckles faded, the conversation lulled. Grace dipped down and removed her leather-bound notebook from its place in her bag. She cracked the notebook open, poised her pen, and gazed around. Soon enough, the inspiration she'd been hoping for struck. She began jotting down any and every detail she took in around them.

The sleigh slid smoothly across the snow, but not smoothly enough for scrawling down ideas as the sun sank lower. Still, she needed to take advantage of what light was left.

She wrote of the magic in the air around them as if it really existed. And how the elven heroine of her story was fast falling for her handsome guide, who happened to have dark hair, chocolate brown eyes, an insanely muscular physique, and a voice to rival the musical chimes of the forest's quiet solace.

Boone peered at her. "You're on a ride like this and spending it all in a notebook?"

"Oh, I'm taking in more than you know," she said, still scribbling, entranced by the scenery around her.

"What kind of research are you doing?"

"I'm a writer." She couldn't bring herself to call herself an author. That would mean she was successfully published, and that hadn't happened yet.

The admission made her think of the gushy thoughts she'd written about Boone before she left the inn. Foolish, stupid, impulsive words. She was tempted to scratch out every one of them. She should never have been so specific that they were about herself and Boone. She wasn't here to live a fantasy. Only to write about fantastic worlds.

Before she could turn the page to find those words again, a spray of snow trickled from overhead, dusting onto her nose and cheeks and catching the light at just the right angle. A melodic sound floated through the sparkly air, sending chills down her back that were more distinctive than the cold already surrounding her. Grace lowered her pen, her back going rigid. "What was that?"

"Whoa," Boone said, pulling on the horse's reins. The jingling bells quietened.

"Do you hear it?" she asked, bracing a hand on the back of the sleigh to peer behind.

He rotated more, head cocked and ears peeled for the sound. "I'm not sure. Is that...music?"

A melody rode on the air with a swirling sound, soft enough to be mistaken for something playing in the distance. Grace checked her phone to see if her writing playlist had accidentally started playing. Nothing. No one else was around, yet the music drifted like a lost descant. Where was it coming from?

Snowflakes picked up speed then. Faster and faster, they flurried. The wind increased, almost abnormally, swirling Grace's hair. A strand caught in her mouth, and she spat it out with a small squeal.

"Where is this coming from?" Boone's voice elevated to match the weather's torrent.

"Is this bad?" she asked.

He squinted, attempting to see through the quickening flurries. "We'd better head back," he said. "I didn't read any signs of a storm this morning, and there weren't any signs in the sky when we left the inn."

He read the sky for signs of upcoming weather? His sexy factor climbed a few notches. Lifting the reins, he guided the horse around. The density of trees made the prospect of a U-turn difficult and instead, they wove through more trees, some Grace didn't perceive until they'd already passed.

With the uptake in wind, the coldness increased, seeping beneath each layer of her skin. The sky grew thicker with snow, the flakes increasing so much it was unbelievable. Was this really how snow worked? Grace tucked her notebook back into her bag and wrapped the blanket tighter around her. She could barely see; she wasn't sure how Boone could.

"Do you know where we're going?" she called.

At the question, keeping the reins in hand, he slowed the

horse to a stop and lifted a hand to shield his eyes as if that would help him see better.

"We're farther out than I thought," he said, squinting. "I don't dare keep riding in this. Hazelnut is scared and could get turned around. We could risk getting lost, which is the last thing either of us wants, especially not this late in the day. The sun will be setting any minute."

Dying in a snowstorm was definitely not part of her book research. A nugget of anxiety nestled beneath her ribs, making her have to work to breathe.

"What do you suggest?" she asked.

He pointed to the left. "I live in the old cottage off the edge of the property. We're not far from it. It's our best bet at this point. We need to seek shelter, and fast. You'll be there alone with me, but at least we can wait out the storm."

Um, wow, holy cow, and every other exclamation her brain could think up. Alone with him? This was a Dickens kind of decision—the best and the worst all in one. He'd been nice to her during this ride, but Grace hadn't forgotten how rude he was the other times before. But she couldn't even see the trees anymore for all the whiteness encircling them. What other option did they have? When night fell, it would get even colder. They needed shelter, fast.

"Okay," she said.

Boone gave her a firm nod as if in agreement, and then called out a command that hopefully the horse understood because Grace didn't. The cold wind whipped at her cheeks and howled its way through the trees. A thousand thoughts whirled through with it. Stupidest of all was the fact that she would be staying the night at his place without any of her things.

Her cute new snowflake pajamas were back at the inn, along with, oh, a toothbrush and toothpaste, to say the least. If she was going to be staying there...with him...the least she could do was make his mouth water.

S top that, she chided herself. Despite their discussion about the word 'romance,' nothing like that was going to happen. They'd find his cottage and wait out the storm. That was all.

Wind tore through the trees. The air was so thick with white, it resembled the lace tablecloth beneath Santa's radio back at the inn.

Minutes—or maybe hours—later, the sleigh slowed in front of a small barn collecting snow on its roof and in the cracks separating its wooden sides. Boone leapt from the sleigh and, arm raised against the flurrying wind, attempted to unhitch Hazelnut from the rig.

Bag in hand, Grace leapt out onto the snow as well. She sank to her shins, and cold snow seeped in through the tops of her boots, which were proving to be more for fashion than functionality the longer she wore them. "Can I help?" she asked.

"See if you can get that barn door open," he called, working with the jingle bells dangling from Hazelnut's leather straps.

Grace had never been around horses, let alone barns, but she circled about and lifted her knees high enough to take the few steps to the barn door. A long board sat across two holds. She rotated the board, swinging it upward—essentially unlocking the door—and attempted to pull it open. Snow packed on the ground. She pulled harder, kicking snow away, clearing as much as she could. Wind fought the door closed every time, pushing against her with such a strong force it stole her breath. After several tries, she finally cleared a triangle of space enough to brace the door open.

White snowflakes collected on Boone's eyebrows and in his

lashes. Grace wondered if hers were the same. He guided Hazelnut past with a hand on the horse's bridle. A gust of wind attempted to close the door, threatening to slam it shut, but Grace dug her frigid heels into the snow and fought to keep the door open until the horse was inside.

12

The door's heavy slam was deafening. Howling wind wailed at being shut out, but Grace exhaled, grateful they'd made it. Taking a few moments to catch her breath, she attempted to peer through the darkened barn. A small amount of light offered outlines of two wooden stalls, and the rafters high overheard fluttered with disturbed birds.

The air was slightly warmer, only because the wind was no longer assailing her, and the barn smelled of hay and manure.

Light through the window was fading fast. Boone guided Hazelnut into one of the stalls. "It's okay, girl," he said by way of comfort to the hesitant horse. The creature showed trust, her ears flicking, and she obeyed, allowing him to step out and close the stall door behind him.

He moved through the darkness and flicked a light switch, but nothing happened.

"Dang it," he said. "Power's out."

Grace glanced around, up to the high rafters and what looked like a hayloft, and then to the stall and the bucket of feed Boone was currently readying. She was surprised he had electricity this far out here at all. She also didn't want to sound like a total snob, but when he said 'cottage' this wasn't exactly what she pictured.

"Just getting Hazelnut settled in and then we'll trudge our way over to the house," he explained over his shoulder. With the bucket ready, he reentered her stall.

"Is it close by?" she asked.

"Just next door," he assured her. "It was hard to see in that blizzard out there."

That was a relief. Grace watched as he carefully removed Hazelnut's bit and bridle. He then relieved the horse of her tack, brushed her down, and placed a woven blanket on her back.

"There's a good girl," he said, patting the horse with a gentle hand. After his gruffness over the radio and the box she'd dropped, and the way he'd snapped and stormed from the room, Grace had suspected he was all prickles. But he'd been gentle and kind when speaking to the little girl that first day. And their conversation during this sleigh ride today, his quick thinking in the danger of the storm, and the care he was taking of his horse led her to believe there was more to Boone than what he showed. What made him be so calloused one moment and kind another? Maybe it was as she'd suspected before. Maybe he'd just been having a rocky few days and was back to his normal self.

"It'll be a rough night," he told the horse. "But all storms pass, and you'll be safe in here, girl."

The horse released a chuff and blinked at him with wary eyes.

"I can tell you take good care of her," Grace said.

Boone kept his back to her, his attention on the mare. He rubbed his knuckles along the horse's jaw and rested his other hand on her forehead. "Yeah, well. She's a good horse. Always has been."

This time he rotated and sniffed. His nose was rosy red, but the traces of snow had blinked away from his lashes. Wind slashed against the barn's sturdy exterior, and the two of them listened to it for a few more minutes before Boone spoke. "We'll have to leave the sleigh out there and unbury it in the morning once this all dies down," he said.

"Will it be okay out there?"

"It'll be fine." He sniffed and raised his gaze to the rafters as if trying to see the wind ravaging the barn's boards. "This old place has withstood many storms."

After ensuring Hazelnut was fed and that she had plenty of water in her trough, Boone secured his hat. "Ready to head back out there?" he asked.

Grace wasn't exactly warm, but she did appreciate the barn's shelter from the wailing wind and whirling snow. But his cottage would undoubtedly be more comfortable than this. It probably smelled better too.

"Ready when you are," she said. Joining his side, she helped to push the barn door open wide enough for each of them to squeeze through. The wind had changed direction, making the barn door too stubborn to close this time, where before closing had been all it wanted to do.

"Push!" Boone shouted. Feet deep in snow, Grace braced her hands against the door's edge and pushed with her might. Together, they were finally able to get it to shut.

"Hopefully, we won't have to dig too much to get it back open in the morning," he shouted through the storm. "Come on."

Boone pointed toward the left where a small but sturdy stone cottage peeked through the snow's swirling flurries. To her surprise, he captured her gloved hand with his. The gesture plunged right through her stomach. He tugged her along through the shin-deep snow, helping her until they stomped through snow collected against the cottage's front door. Grace helped clear the drift, and soon they were inside.

Once more, the wind was shut out, and this time its whirling howls didn't quite penetrate the cottage's thick stone walls the way it had the barn's thinner boards. Darkness greeted them. The sun had nearly fully set.

"We made it," Grace said gratefully, breathless. She was ready to sink onto the cottage floor. Between fear of frostbite and getting lost in said frozen circumstances, and the adrenaline and energy pumping through her as a result of getting Hazelnut into the barn and making their way through more snow than she'd ever stood in, her body was beyond weary.

"That we did." Boone removed his hat and gloves. He parted a pair of curtains more feminine than Grace would have expected a rugged man like him to have in his home, allowing a sliver of fading silver light through. "And none too soon."

He left the curtains open. Darkness was collecting fast, accentuating the snow's bright gusts. Grace removed her thin gloves, which were soaked clear through. Her fingers were icicles. She set her snow-drenched bag on the carpet and blew warm air onto her icy fingers. "Where did this storm come from?" The sky earlier had been completely cloudless.

The memory of the floating melody hanging in the air around them refused to leave her alone. The music sounded exactly like what she'd heard before she'd found that necklace in her room. Why would she have heard it out in the forest? She waited for Boone to bring it up—she *knew* he'd heard it too.

Boone removed his coat. He sat at the small, round dining table just off from the door and began to unlace his heavy-duty boots. "I'm not sure." Then he glanced her way. Grace hadn't moved from her spot on the rug. Snow still clustered on her heels and her pants were as soaked as everything else on her was. Her chin juddered from sheer coldness.

She could just hear Dad's voice now, griping about having to wade through piles of snow to get to school in the mornings and how cold he ended up being on a permanent basis until spring arrived. She'd never completely understood how someone could be that cold...until now.

"Please," Boone said, gesturing to the chair across from him. "Have a seat. I know it's not much, but at least we'll be warm in here once I get a fire going."

"Thanks," Grace said. "And actually, it's really cute and cozy in here." She took the opportunity to glance around the dim space as she sat. A small living area on one side with an old couch and a rocking chair by the quiet fireplace stocked with fresh logs. A kitchen with a small, outdated stove and a mini fridge nesting on a short counter to the other.

Though she couldn't see everything through the shadows, the décor was dated at best, nothing coordinated or staged for anything but functionality. The pictures on the wall were mostly painted landscapes or old black and white photographs of people behind discolored glass.

One thing was extremely lacking, however, considering the season. "No Christmas tree?" she asked, sliding her feet from her useless boots. She wiggled her toes just to make sure she still could. She was really looking forward to that fire he mentioned.

"No," Boone said, rising to retrieve something from a drawer in the kitchen behind him. He returned with a towel to mop up the snow that had puddled on the floor. Grace rose to help, amazed that her feet could hold her weight with how cold they were. Her jaw chattered again, but she clenched her teeth in attempt to make it be still.

"I don't do Christmas," he added.

"How do you not *do* Christmas?" Her words were stilted, coming out with more interruption thanks to her chattering jaw.

Boone eyed her. "You're freezing," he said, not answering her question. "Let's get a fire going. You can lay your wet things near it so they dry out. I've got some clothes you can change into if you'd like. I also have space heaters, but with the electricity out..."

"A fire will be great," she said. Every part of her was cold, from her fingertips to the spaces where her ribs met her spine. She was cold in places she didn't even know she could be.

He tossed a few more logs into the brick fireplace and within minutes a fire was going. There went another sexy notch in her mental calculations. He was really racking up those points. Little by little, he was transitioning from Demon Boone back to book boyfriend material. Sexiness and manly know-how were written in his genetics. Grace shook the thoughts away as heat from the fire seeped into her frosty skin, melting the ice from her fingertips.

Boone stepped out once more, through a door she hadn't noticed, and returned minutes later with what looked like flannel pants and an old sweatshirt with a bear on it. Grace didn't really want to step away from the fire long enough to change, but he showed her to the bathroom. Soon, she was wearing his clothes that smelled like fresh laundry, and she laid her wet pants, socks, and gloves in front of the fire.

"How long have you lived here?" Grace asked, placing the last of her socks on the floor in front of the hearth. She held her hands to the flames. Heat was quickly pouring into the room and she was glad to have a little more light to see by.

Boone had also changed into a pair of comfortable, plaid pants, a fresh T-shirt that said, "West Hills, Montana," and thick socks.

"My whole life." He slid the rocking chair forward so she could sit and warm her hands and feet. Grace sat gratefully. "I grew up here. So did my dad, and his." He gestured to the old pictures sitting on the fireplace. "Junie grew up at the inn. We're not just cousins; we've been friends our whole lives, too."

Grace remembered seeing the painting of this cottage in the

inn's front room. "This is the little cottage in that painting back at the inn."

"Yes, ma'am, it is." He sank onto the couch, either not needing to warm his hands like she did, or not wanting to push her away. How was he not freezing? Here she was practically hogging the fire.

Shortly, the fire's heat filled the room. In a space this confined, it was hardly a wonder. Boone prepared a small dinner for them of fish from his freezer and some green beans from a jar that Junie and her mom had canned the previous summer. Both were delicious. He then heated water for hot cocoa and passed her a mug. Grace sat at his dining table across from him, soaking the mug's heat into her hands. The warm liquid stirred in her belly. And outside, snow continued swirling.

"Looks like I won't be making it home for Christmas after all," she said, not bothered in the slightest. Deep down, she'd been hoping for some reason to stay to reveal itself. A reason that wouldn't make her seem like the world's worst daughter and sister. She would miss getting to see Stephanie and meet her cute baby, but there would be other times too. Maybe once Grace got a book deal, she could afford to fly out to Florida.

She retrieved her phone, but wherever the cell towers were located, they must have been affected by the storm too. She had no service here whatsoever. She'd have to let Mom know about her unexpected roadblock later.

Boone sipped his cocoa. "Even if you and I hadn't gone out, you wouldn't have made it back to town for your flight. They close the pass during bad storms like this. It's not safe for anyone to go through."

Grace hadn't thought of that. She remembered driving along the narrow, winding, mountain road in the back of her Uber driver's car. "At least I'll have a good excuse to tell my mother."

"I know it's none of my business," Boone said, lowering his

mug and kicking back to stretch his legs across the thin carpet, "but I thought you were heading home to meet a guy."

"That was part of it."

"You don't seem all that put out about missing it."

Grace took another sip of warm chocolate and sorted out the easiest explanation. "My mom invited him to meet me during our annual family Christmas dinner. She wanted to set me up."

He raised a single brow. "Sounds like you'll be missing a hot date."

Or she'd found a better alternative. Grace wasn't about to say that out loud. She cradled the warm mug in her hands. "Nothing that I was looking forward to. I am going to miss out meeting my sister's new baby. I haven't seen my sister in a few years, not since before she had her. I didn't know they were planning on coming home when I made this trip."

"That's too bad," Boone said. "I haven't seen my brother for a while either."

"The real estate brother?"

Boone nodded. "He travels a lot for his job, stays until the fix and flips are done, and then heads to the next project. He's never in one place long enough for me to visit."

"Do you miss him?" Grace asked.

"Sometimes," Boone said. "Yeah, I do, I guess."

"I miss my sister too. I called her when I found out they were coming, before I rescheduled my flight. She told me she was okay if I stayed here, but from the sound of her voice, I know she really wanted me home celebrating Christmas with my family instead of being here alone in the mountains. She probably didn't realize it until I was already gone or something."

"But you want to be here alone in the mountains?"

"Yeah," she said. "I do."

"Because the view is gorgeous?" he asked.

Grace fought the smile this statement brought. He couldn't possibly know he'd included himself in that statement. "Yes."

"Where it's completely solitary, and where Santa Claus himself is rumored to have stopped by a hundred years ago?"

Grace puzzled this for a few moments. "Yes." Harper's Inn did claim to be America's North Pole, after all.

"Then what's the problem?"

She released a sigh and placed her mug on the table. "I feel like—I don't know, like I'm letting my family down somehow by not being there for them."

"You got kids wanting to spend Christmas with you?"

"No, I'm not married." Smooth, Grace. Real smooth.

He sat up a little straighter and leaned toward her across the table. "Then who are you disappointing? Really?"

"I don't know," she said, appreciating his insightful questions and the opportunity to purge this to someone who wasn't her mother. "It's the principle of the thing. My parents insisted they were okay with me coming here, but then Mom talked me out of it. And she's right. Christmas should be spent with family."

The light left his eyes. "Sounds to me like Christmas should be spent how you need to spend it."

There was an edge to Boone's voice that made Grace suspect he wasn't referring to her at all. She was dying to ask him what he'd meant earlier about not *doing* Christmas, but she found she couldn't. She wanted him to open up to her because he wanted to.

"You're a grown, strong woman with books to write and places to go. It's okay for your mom to accept that."

Grace was stunned. Where was this coming from? "Thank you," was all she could manage to say.

"Anytime. Christmas is no excuse for people to meddle where they don't belong. It's your life. You need to live it in the best way for you."

This selfishness he expressed sounded so contradictory to the man he'd shown himself to be. Grace mustered her courage and asked what she'd been dying to for minutes now. "Is that why you don't have a tree? You don't celebrate Christmas?"

He placed a hand on the table beside his mug. Discomfort punctured his expression, and he glanced away. "No. I don't celebrate Christmas. Not anymore."

Grace wanted so badly to ask every other nosy question pouring through her, but whatever happened to him was clearly difficult. He was so kind to let her into his home, to share his food and give her warm, dry clothes and a place to stay. She couldn't tread on his generous hospitality any more than she had. But oh, come all ye faithful, she wanted to.

Boone cleared his throat. "Anyway. We should probably crash. Let me show you where you'll be sleeping."

Grace had passed a single bedroom on her way to change clothes. She hadn't seen any others, nor had she noticed any stairs. She guessed where he was headed. "Boone, I can't take your bed."

"Nonsense," he said. "This place has only ever had one bedroom, and tonight it's all yours."

"I can't do that. Where will you sleep? That couch looks pretty cozy. I'm fine sleeping there."

"What kind of host would I be if I took the bed and left you to the couch? I insist."

With reluctance, she followed him toward the closed door across from the couch. The minute they stepped through it, a block of cold air smacked straight into her. It was like they were back outside all over again.

Grace inhaled through her teeth. "Brr," she said, rubbing her arms.

Boone clicked on a flashlight, and a bright beam speared

light through the small room. "Sorry, it's much colder in here," he said. "But once you get in the covers, you'll warm right up."

She doubted that.

The bed had an unpolished log frame and several patchwork quilts atop it. It had been nicely made, with the blankets arranged and folded at the top beneath the single pillow. Good gracious, he only had one pillow. Was she going to use that too?

"You make your bed even when you're not expecting company?" she asked.

"My mom always insisted." He shrugged. "It's become a habit."

She imagined him as a small boy, careful to make his bed before leaving for school. Then again, if he'd grown up clear out here, had he gone to school? "Was this your room growing up?" she asked.

"Hm?"

"You said you grew up here. I just wondered...well, where?" There was just the one room in this cottage. How big was his family?

"Oh, I guess for me, saying 'here,' means here on the property," he said with an apologetic grimace. "I didn't grow up in this cottage. I lived at the inn. They added on the spa and a few more rooms when I was in high school. I had my own room there."

"Was it an inn then, too?"

"It was," he said. "Another reason Mom insisted the beds be made. She was in charge of room service and preparing the bedding—and then passed that job on to Junie before she died. I helped my dad fix things and spent most of my time out in the barn or romping through the hills outside."

"Why does that not surprise me?" No wonder he knew where everything was around here. Grace didn't miss the fact that his mom had died. With his brother so far away, he really was alone out here.

He chuckled. "You know, back in the day, my great-grandparents raised eight kids in this place." His voice was quiet in the stillness. Wind whipped against the windowpanes, and Grace was beyond grateful to be in here, out of its path.

"Eight? Where did they all sleep?" She and Boone could barely stand in here without colliding. She couldn't imagine eight people in this tiny room.

"Together," he said, gesturing to the bed. An awkward pause stood between them.

Grace wasn't sure what to say, so instead, she took in the books on a shelf that protruded from the wall and his tidy dresser, devoid of anything on its surface. Everything was so bare, as if he wanted to keep this place the way it had been back then. Aside from a few cowboy hats hanging on the wall, nothing in here really spoke of his personality or interests.

It was almost as though he didn't want to settle. But if he lived here, that didn't really make sense. What was he hiding himself from?

Boone cleared his throat. "I'll just—"

"Oh, right." Grace moved toward the bed in attempt to leave space by the door. Unwittingly, Boone stepped in the same direction. They collided.

The brush of his body against hers sent a shot of awareness over her. Grace's balance teetered. She could have sworn his hand came up around her only to be quickly jerked back. Warmth coursed through her at the feel of his chest against hers, making her momentarily forget the room's cold temperature.

His gaze trapped hers. "Sorry," he said, swallowing. "I was just getting a blanket."

Grace ducked back, knocking into the dresser and biting her tongue. "Sure, I'm sorry too."

He dipped his head and bent beneath the bed, shining the

flashlight. Then, he stood with a thick quilt under his arm and placed the flashlight on the bed. "I'll leave this here in case you need it." Its beam projected toward the wall, leaving shadows to play on Boone's features.

"Thank you," she said.

He bobbed his head and stepped away, toward the door. "Well, then. Good night, Grace."

"Good night, Boone. Thank you for all your help."

He smiled and closed the door, shutting out both heat and light and leaving her alone.

13

———

Grace drew back the sheets, her body humming at the idea of sleeping where Boone usually did. Clicking off the flashlight, she slipped into the bed.

The sheets were like plunging into a frozen river. While part of her body warmed beneath the blankets, that warmth refused to spread to her toes and heels. Even her shoulders shivered. Try as she might, she couldn't make herself get any warmer. She rubbed her feet against each other, feeling the friction in the moment, but once she stopped, they went back to being cold.

She always had the opposite problem in Arizona. Everything was so blasted hot. She usually relished the feeling of stepping inside and out of the soul-crushing heat.

"I'll never look at air conditioning the same way again," she muttered to the silence. Again, she waited, huddling her limbs in close, waiting for the promised warmth to spread and allow her to relax. But the longer she lay there, the colder she grew.

Grace fluttered her lips. Boone was being a generous host, but this wasn't working. Though she couldn't see snow collecting at the windowsill, the wind continued howling outside, and the sound instilled yet more cold into her. It was as though the cold had gone bone deep, falling into the inside of her where heat couldn't penetrate.

She'd love that hut tub back at Harper's Inn right about now...

Shivering, Grace sat up. Movement was her best chance of generating heat now. Unless the fire was still going in the front room? Maybe Boone would be willing to trade places. Light gleamed from beneath the door, so she decided to chance it.

Heat instantly enveloped her the minute she opened the door. Boone was settled on the couch beneath the quilt he'd retrieved, wearing a pair of glasses and reading a book by firelight.

"Hey, there," he said in surprise, lowering his book.

"This room is much warmer than that one," she said by way of explanation. "You wear glasses?"

"Only to read by," he said. "And yes, this place gets a little drafty. I don't mind it; I'm always hot when I sleep."

Grace snorted. She was sure his schedule for hotness wasn't limited to sleep alone.

"Boy, that sounded like a brag, didn't it?" He pulled at his neck.

She stepped toward the fire. Heat combatted the cold inside her, but the embers weren't as full and flickering as before.

"I wasn't going to say it," she said.

"Go ahead, say it."

"Okay, you're hot."

He laughed and shook his head. "That's not what I meant. You were supposed to tell me I'm full of myself."

"Are you full of yourself?" She hadn't gotten that vibe. Distant and closed-off, maybe. Rude at times. But not cocky.

"Only when I'm trying to make myself sound better than I am."

She rubbed her arms, wishing the fire was at its full force as before. "Sorry, I just—I'm not used to this much *cold*. It never drops like this down where I'm from. It's like, seeped into my bones."

Boone pressed his lips together, his forehead pinched in concentration. After several long moments, he resituated, lowered his feet to the floor, and lifted the blanket from his lap. "Come on over here," he said.

Grace went rigid. "You mean, sit with you?"

"Yes, I do. I'm about to brag about myself again, but I have heard somewhere that two bodies nestled together can create more heat side by side than one person alone."

"I've heard that too," Grace hedged.

His brows lifted. "Care to test the theory? It's better than you shivering all night long. I'd never forgive myself if you lost toes on my watch."

She chewed her lower lip. This was the last thing she'd expected from him, and it was *not* why she'd come out here. But she couldn't deny how tempting his offer was. Was this wise, getting so close to him?

Guess it was time to find out.

She took his offer. She tiptoed across the room, did an ungraceful pirouette, and nestled close to his side. Boone placed the blanket over them both and draped his arm around her shoulder.

The man was an oven, a blaze all on his own. His proximity warmed her instantly, making her want to sink in and settle there. She released a relieved moan and tucked in against him.

"Won't I make you cold now?"

"Not possible," he said, rubbing her arm. "I'm hot, remember?"

She laughed again. Being this close to him was comfortable, more than she thought it would be. He was strong and warm and secure. She stared at the fire's red embers peeking through the remaining chunks of blackened wood. Cold slowly dissipated from within her and became replaced with something else.

"How's your book?" she asked, gesturing to the volume he'd placed on the table beside him. She couldn't see the title.

"It's good."

Silence. The same silence that had swirled between them right before he'd apologized to her in the sleigh. Grace reveled in the memory of that apology and his impressive behavior since. She basked in the sensation of his touch, of his arm around her and the pulsing energy building between them.

"You know," she said. "Even despite the cold, I still love it."

"Love what?"

"Snow. I wish I could take some home with me. More than that, I wish I didn't have to go home. I've never been to a place like this before. To a place that makes me feel like this."

"Like what?" His velvet voiced strummed her senses.

"That it's okay to slow down. To breathe and enjoy the scenery." Not to mention being held by Boone while his fingers stroked her arm.

"Where do you work?" he asked.

"At a call center. We sell homeopathic cleaning products and natural remedies, that kind of thing. I'm always inside; it's too hot to do much outside in nature. And the desert has its own kind of beauty, but with woods like these? I think I'd like to get lost even without the snow."

"That's why I'm here," Boone said, speaking as though he hadn't meant to.

Her heart drummed a little harder. "Why? To get lost? You seemed to know exactly where you were going out there."

He stared off for a few moments and then seemed to shake away whatever dark thought plagued him. When he spoke, it was to change the subject. "You said you're writing something? What are you writing?"

Grace leaned her head against his shoulder. Her warming limbs allowed her to relax against him that much more. "I'm working on a fantasy novel. You know. Elves. Castles. Magic. I like fantasy."

"I do too," he said. "Are you going to let me read what you've been writing?" His hand continued to stroke her arm.

"Um, no?"

He laughed, but she was dead serious. She couldn't let him see that half of her descriptions were daydreams about him and the other half called him a demon.

"Grace." His voice was full of hesitation.

"Yes?"

"About my apology earlier—"

"It's okay," she said, wanting to assure him again. She wanted him to know she was completely okay with this turn of events. "Really. I'm not at my best all the time either."

He chuckled. "You're being extremely kind," he said. "But I will say I'm not myself this time of year."

"Why not?" she asked.

He lowered his head and sniffed, shaking his head as though he didn't want to answer. "That is a complicated answer."

"We have a while," she said. "If you're willing. But if you're not, it's okay."

He leaned his head against hers, surprising her. Her breath hitched, catching in her chest. His face was so close to hers now. His fingers ceased roving over hers, and he held her hand in his.

Grace thrilled at his touch. This was no mere effort to keep her warm. This was a connection, an inclusion of her, almost as if he needed the reassurance of her touch as much as she needed his. His fingers stroked the sides of hers, trailing to their tips and back.

"I was married once," he said. "We lived in Deer Lodge. My wife was a nurse, and I did some custom farming for a local farmer. He hired me to run his equipment for him during harvest. I did other odd jobs here and there, and we got by."

"What happened?" Grace was almost afraid to ask, but she voiced the question anyway. "Did you get divorced?" Was that why he was hiding up here? He'd said he lived here for a few years.

"Amy was pregnant. She got hit by a car."

Grace's hands flew to her mouth. She gasped and moved away from him so she could see his face. "Boone, I'm so sorry."

Pain lingered in his eyes. He cast his gaze to the empty rocking chair. "I lost them both that night. And I knew I couldn't stay there in our apartment where traces of her were everywhere I turned. I'd grown up here in West Hills, and no one else in my family was living up at the cottage anymore. Junie's mom, who owns the property, signed the cottage over to me, no questions asked."

Grace rested a hand on his arm. "Boone, that's heartbreaking. I'm so sorry. How long ago was that?"

He inhaled, long and deep. She felt his chest expand against hers. "We were young. I moved to work on a ranch just out of high school and she and I married a few years later. About three years ago now. Junie has tried getting me to date, but you're the first woman I've really even touched since." He stroked her hands only once more before closing his fingers around hers.

Time stilled then. Heat from his touch expanded into her chest and gave her heart a few extra beats. Their eyes locked, and her breath lodged into her throat.

"I'm honored," Grace said sincerely.

To be touched by a man like Boone was something to be cherished. Suddenly, the pieces of his erratic behavior began to make sense. She could understand why this time of year was so hard for him and why he'd been so on edge. It sounded like he didn't give his attention lightly, though she couldn't fathom what it was about her that made him want to change his isolation streak.

"What about you?" he asked. "You said you're not married. Have you ever been?"

She shook her head. "No. I don't date all that much either. I don't meet many guys while being boxed in at that call center. I just sit at a desk and talk to strangers who want to buy stuff our company offers or who have problems with their existing products."

"Have you ever thought of leaving?" he asked. "Of doing something else?"

"I want to so badly. That's why I'm writing. I know a lot of other authors don't make a living off their books, but some do, and I intend on being one of them." She could hear the longing in her voice even as she expressed the sentiment.

"And who's the guy your mom was trying to set you up with? Do you like him?"

Boone's hand released hers. Grace flicked her eyes up to meet his. His attention was fully on her. With the care used for handling delicate things, he brushed a hair away from her face.

Grace drowned in the intimate change of his touch. Her lids fluttered, and she struggled to concentrate on his question. "I'm not a fan of blind dates," she managed to say, though her voice was breathy.

While the room grew darker from the fading firelight, amusement gleamed in Boone's eyes. "I don't know anyone who is," he said. He visibly swallowed. A question fluctuated in his expression before he voiced it. "So...you don't know the man you were supposed to be meeting?"

His head tilted. His eyes flicked to her mouth.

"No," she breathed.

He placed his other hand on the side of her neck and inched in. "You aren't dating him?"

Her heart gave a frantic chug. "No."

"Then you won't mind if I kiss you?" His lids half-lowered, the gleam in his eyes turning sultry and ravenous all at once.

Grace's fingertips tingled. She couldn't speak. Her gaze was trapped in his. Her lips parted, allowing breath passage. He moved in closer and guided her chin upward just enough.

She pounded inside with the anticipation of feeling his lips on hers. Worry and want both warred inside her. Worry that she wouldn't be any good at this. Wanting him so badly she could hardly process a single thought.

With acceptance, and slow deliberation, she let her lids close completely, giving him her wordless answer.

She felt his breath coax her skin, sensed him edging ever nearer. And then his lips touched hers. Just a brushstroke, as gentle as a wave upon the sand. The pressure was light enough to tease but present enough to make her want more.

She didn't want to take too much too soon. Grace let him lead, resting her hands on his chest as his hands cradled her face and he allowed his lips to introduce themselves. They pressed once, twice, three times in gentle motion. And the third time they lingered. The intensity changed then. Boone gathered her to his chest. She wove her fingers into his hair, allowing him to turn and press her into the couch as he parted her mouth with his.

Grace wanted this kiss to envelop her. She wanted to do nothing but this for as long as they could. But they were alone here, and considering all that snow outside, they might be alone for a good long while. And even though she craved it, she couldn't let herself or him get too carried away.

This time, she took the lead, savoring the taste of his lips and slowing the tempo.

He angled his head, familiarizing his mouth with hers. Her entire body lit up with his every touch, illuminating her awareness and luring her in like a hypnotic song. His lips were velvet, his hands were harnesses, and she felt herself wanting to cave, to burrow in this exact place and stay for a while.

Gradually, the kiss slowed. Grace let her mouth linger, relishing the feel of his against hers, intaking his breath, feeling his pulse rattle, before drawing away again to find his eyes smoldering and his mouth smirking in an inquisitive kind of way.

Heaven help her.

"Wow," she said with a breath, sitting back, needing the space between them.

"What?"

"You...This...I just...Tonight has been so magical. Like something from a story, and I want to make sure we don't take things to a place we'll regret."

"You're right." He fidgeted and stole a glance at her, looking devastatingly handsome. "We won't."

He smiled that dimple-teasing smile, stroked her cheek, and pressed another kiss to her mouth. Each time, his kisses were more decadent than the last, to the point that Grace was growing ever more certain she could thoroughly enjoy kissing him for the rest of her life.

"I don't know what's happening to me," he muttered against her mouth.

"No?"

"No," he said, his lips whisper-soft, skimming the surface of hers before dipping in a little bit deeper. "You came out of nowhere and I haven't been the same since."

"Me neither," she said, deciding to be honest. "You've been on my mind since the moment we met."

He cradled her face and released a low laugh. "I find that hard to believe, unless you're referring to my treatment of you. I wasn't the nicest guy on the planet. I can see why you couldn't stop thinking of the nasty sleigh driver."

She smiled. "I didn't say you were always nice. In fact, I was ready to make you a villain in my book."

His rumbling laugh erupted from his chest. "My completely charming personality give you that impression? I think I'd make a pretty remarkable villain."

"You'd make a remarkable anything. Even if you are on the naughty list."

He reared back at this, a full smile teasing his lips this time. "Is that what you'd call me? Naughty?"

"Well, you're not exactly on the nice list."

"How about now?"

He didn't give her the chance to answer but instead stole a few more kisses. She let him, soaking in every sensation and thoroughly enjoying the banter he interjected in between.

He pulled away but allowed his gaze to rest on her face. She held her breath captive in her lungs, refused to set it free. Her heart was a rabbit's hind foot, hammering against her ribs. She could go on like this all night, kissing him, chattering playfully in between, but something told her that would be a very bad idea.

His thumbs stroked her jaw. "Excuse me, Grace, but I think I'd better go sleep in my room and let you have the couch. Are you warm enough now?" His smile lingered, though this time it didn't reach his eyes. It mingled with just a hint of pain. Grace couldn't figure out what might be causing such a look.

Warm enough—that was an understatement if she'd ever heard one. What just happened between them? And how had it happened?

"I—I am."

He sat up. Carefully, he gathered her hands to his lips and placed a kiss on the back of the hand nearest him before stand-

ing. She straightened as well, feeling a small wave of sheepish-
ness at how they'd gone from sitting side by side to...that.

"All right, then. Good night."

She didn't want him to leave. She wanted to reach for him, to
keep his hands with hers, to convince him he could stay a little
longer. But he was right to go. She'd had enough confusion from
him to last a lifetime.

That didn't mean she didn't want more, and from the way his
smoldering eyes kept glancing at her, so did he.

Yes, this would be better if he left.

With a final glance and a nod, he stepped through the door,
closing it behind him and leaving her alone in his front room.

Grace stared at the door for a long time, lost in thought. This
entire day had been one helping of unexpected after another.
He'd been civility and kindness during their sleigh ride. He'd
acted fast, getting them to safety. He'd fed her, gave her cocoa,
offered her his room, and then when she told him she was cold,
he invited her in closer than she ever dreamed.

And his kisses. Traces of him still lingered, not only on her
lips, but in her bloodstream, spiking her pulse with his name in
every beat. Still. He'd mentioned getting carried away. What did
that mean? Was he saying he'd only kissed her because of their
snowed-in situation?

Trapped in this adorable cottage in the middle of a snowstorm the day before Christmas Eve? What could be more
romantic than that?

The truth was, they were both caught up in the moment.
They'd been sitting too close to each other. Sense had gone out
the window along with the storm outside, that was all it had
been.

She couldn't believe that, no matter how many times she
repeated it to herself. Her heart wouldn't let her. If she were
being honest, this side of Boone made so much more sense than

any of the other interactions she'd had with him before. He was kind. Helpful, thoughtful, and had been so honest about his wife and baby. How devastating that must have been for him. No wonder he wanted to hide himself away from the world.

And the fact that he told her she was the first woman he'd touched since his wife? Was that true? Had kissing her been difficult for him at all? Maybe that was why he'd excused himself, but she was glad he had. They needed more time together if this was going to go any further.

Grace nestled onto the couch and pulled the blanket over her, watching the fire's dying embers and burning inside right along with them. She had been cold before, but while the room was colder and emptier without him, a little flame all its own burned inside her heart.

She'd had him completely wrong. He was so not the villain. Not after a kiss and an evening like that. Grace was determined to make him her hero.

14

————

Boone lay in his bed and stared at the dark ceiling for a long time, listening to the wind. His heart paced in his chest as he remembered how good it felt to hold Grace close, to have her in his arms. To kiss her.

The mellow tone of her voice refused to leave his brain. But temptation was about right. That's all it had been. The two of them closed in here during a storm like this? With her as striking and lovely as she was, with their conversation coming so easily, with her body so close to his—the guard he worked so hard to maintain had completely crumbled.

He'd opened up to her. Said things he never should have said. Done things he never should have done. Yet, it took everything in him not to go back out there and kiss her again.

He rolled onto his side, hoping a new position would be the key to relaxing, to drifting off. Grace's comments about her job wouldn't leave him alone either. What kind of life would that be, to sit at a desk all day and talk to strangers on the phone? She clearly wasn't happy doing it.

He shouldn't care what she was happy doing. He should

never have let her in, and now that she'd wriggled her way into his brain, she wouldn't leave.

Boone grunted and tried his other side. He hoped the snow was manageable in the morning. He had to get Grace out of his personal space. He'd never seen a storm pick up the way this one had. And the melody in the air just before the weather started its tantrum...

"No way." Boone bolted upright, inhaling. Junie had said the radio had been meddling in others' love lives. Even her own. Santa's radio couldn't be the reason for the storm. What other explanation was there for the melody both he and Grace had heard, though?

There was nothing for it. He meant when he said he believed. He'd been told the story enough times it had become gospel truth. Was Santa out there somewhere, spying on them? Interfering with their lives?

Just because Boone didn't celebrate Christmas anymore didn't mean he no longer revered the Christ child or feel St. Nick existed. He'd simply done away with the fripperies and over-done extravaganza of trees and reindeer, of gifts and bows and music. Amy had loved all of that. She would go overboard turning their apartment into a shrine to all things red and green. Paper-cut snowflakes dangling from the ceiling, twinkling lights in the windows, cinnamon sticks and pine-scented candles.

She'd been wrapping presents for days, piling them around the tree overladen with huge, shining bulbs that took up half of their tiny living room.

"Why are you wrapping the baby's clothes?" Boone had asked when he'd come home from work one day and caught her wrapping a pair of tiny pink booties. He hadn't bothered fighting his amusement at the sight. Amy sat on the floor, but her belly was so round she could barely bend forward to cut the paper. "The baby won't be here to open them yet."

Amy rested a hand on her swollen stomach that looked more like she'd stuffed a watermelon under her shirt. "I may still have two months left," she'd said, "but if you could feel what I feel with how she moves around, you'd know our Baby Grace is already here."

She secured the piece of tape on the last bit of paper she'd folded around the booties.

Boone's heart ached at the memory. Losing his wife had been like nothing he'd ever experienced. It was as though he'd been drawn and quartered in the medieval sense, left alive while his insides were cut right from his chest. He'd lain beside Amy every night, resting a hand on her stomach to feel their baby kick, talking about the best ways of parenting and arguing over who their little Gracie girl was going to look more like.

Amy had rolled over and smiled that smile he loved. She'd rested her hands on his face. "I hope she looks more like you. You were always better looking."

Boone had stopped her argument with a kiss, holding her tight and bursting with anxious excitement for the day their baby would be born. The day he'd be able to hold the small little girl in his arms as well.

But that day never came. A teenaged boy driving a pickup truck had run a red light because he was texting. He'd slid through the intersection and crashed into the side of Amy's car, killing her instantly. The baby's heartbeat faded in the hospital as the doctors had tried to save her.

Tears pooled in Boone's eyes at the surge of memory. He hurried to wipe them. He wasn't used to allowing so many recollections to resurface at once. He choked back a sob, not wanting to give Grace any indication that he was in here, hurting.

Grace. He closed his eyes. From the minute she'd told him her name back in Harper's Inn the day she arrived, he was determined to keep his distance from her. How could he be anything remotely close to this woman who shared the name he and his late wife were planning on giving their baby daughter? Why—why had he let Grace get so close to him when he knew she couldn't stay that way?

H e rolled again, tucking the blanket closer to his chin. Though it was infantile and stupid, he pulled his legs in closer, needing to keep himself from falling apart. After the accident, after his wife and child had been pronounced dead on Christmas Eve, he'd returned to their empty apartment. The Christmas decorations Amy had taken such care to set out were no longer lively or jubilant, no longer a source of reverence and excitement.

He knocked the tree over in an emotional rage. He tore every strand of light from the windows. He kicked all the presents she'd wrapped into the corner. And he'd crumpled to the floor because he had nothing to keep him upright any longer.

Now every Christmas tree he saw was a reminder that his wife and baby were gone.

He was glad Grace hadn't pressed him about it earlier. Junie kept pestering him to open himself up again, but Boone didn't see how he could. Inviting Grace to share a blanket with him was madness. Telling her about his wife, letting her see into his life, sharing a part of him and kissing her and admitting how she affected him, it had all been a mistake.

Grace was delightful in so many ways—her conversation, her ideas, her delight at small things many others he took on rides failed to notice. She had a sense of humor he could appreciate and a smile that went straight through him. And the way the sunlight brought out gold strands in her hair had made him ache to run his hands through it. Once he'd allowed himself to notice her virtues, they'd been all he could see during their sleigh ride.

That was probably why he'd invited her so close to him in the first place. He'd felt pity for her claim at coldness, for the way she looked so vulnerable with her blonde hair tumbling in waves down her shoulders and in his oversized (for her) clothes.

Sympathy had struck him, and then once he had her in his arms, he'd only wanted her closer. When she wove her fingers through his and shared secrets about her life, when he caught the glittering light in her eyes, when he'd been able to draw in a fuller breath than he'd managed in years, he'd lost his senses altogether.

He'd pushed away the possibility for so long, it hadn't been anywhere close to his grasp. Maybe that was why he'd acted so impulsively being snowed-in here with Grace.

And she'd let him. She'd wanted him—as much as he'd wanted her.

Junie had beat the idea of loving someone again over his head so many times he should have a concussion by now. Her attempts had only caused him irritation and exasperation, but was she right? Was it possible for Boone to allow himself to feel the things Grace was making him feel?

He'd loved Amy with all his heart and soul and everything in between. She had meant more to him than his own life. He wasn't sure he'd fully breathed since the day she died.

Not until earlier. Not until he held Grace.

One tick at a time, he felt his body relax. His legs straight-ened out once more beneath the blanket until they reached the coolest part of the mattress—a sensation he loved. He rolled onto his back and stared up at the ceiling while possibility floated before his eyes.

Could he love again? Could he feel like this? Could he take in full breaths, enjoy the beauty of the forest he used to feel so suffocated by, and smile on top of that? He was fairly sure he'd smiled more today than he had in a long time. Boone hadn't even realized how much his lips were unused to curving upward until they were compelled to do so every time Grace spoke or glanced his way.

He was *alive* with Grace. Boone didn't realize just how much of his time he spent going through the motions until his blood beat like fire in his veins, until he pulsed as if for the first time, until the flicker of light in her eyes and the softness in her smile made him want to never let her go.

It was stupid. It was reckless to put his heart on his sleeve again when he'd kept it locked inside his chest for so long.

He couldn't do that again. Getting closer to Grace now would only end in more heartbreak. He had to keep his distance from here on out. Grace was leaving. She would go back to Arizona. He could go on eking out his fraction of a life. No radio or Christmas magic was going to make him change his mind. Yet, he fell asleep and dreamed of Grace.

15

The next morning, Grace woke to the scent of sizzling bacon and eggs. She stretched her arms and legs, relishing the contentment of a good night's sleep. A fresh fire blazed in the hearth, offering its heat to the room, so when she rose from the couch and left the blanket behind, she was still pleasantly warm.

She wasn't sure when Boone had woken. She didn't hear him start a new fire. But she glanced back at the couch and the blanket they'd shared—the blanket she'd slept under—with new eyes. Did last night really happen? Did he really hold her? Kiss her repeatedly and in such an adorable way? Grace thrilled at the thought. Their kisses had replayed a few times in her dreams, and she was sure the sunrise that morning was still happening *inside* of her.

Boone stood with his back to her in the kitchen, one hand gripping the handle of a skillet on the stove. He was no longer in his pajama pants but fully dressed in jeans and a long-sleeved, red flannel shirt. His hair was wet and tousled, and she thought she detected a scent of his soap. A shower would be nice, but she would have to wait until they got back to the inn for hers.

Still, the thought of getting freshened up wasn't enough to make her want to leave anytime soon. She approached his back and wrapped her arms around him from behind.

"Morning," she said, resting her cheek against his back and detecting his heartbeat. "Thanks for starting the fire. It's nice and warm in here."

He stood stiff and unresponsive for so long Grace's hands slipped. She began to think she'd overstepped. Maybe she'd imagined the change between them the night before. Was she pushing things too far this morning?

A handful of beats passed. Her pulse pounded in her ears, and the distinct sting of rejection overtook her.

Just as she lowered her hands, he snatched them back again and turned to face her. With the spatula in one hand, he brought her hand to his lips.

"Good morning," he said with a soft smirk.

Relief flooded her. The same smile she hadn't been able to clear from her cheeks as she'd replayed their firelight kisses returned. Her heart flapped in her chest and she gratefully cast aside her brief bout of insecurity. "That smells amazing."

Boone returned to the savory bacon strips. "Thanks. We still have no power, but I was able to get the stove lit."

"It pays to have outdated appliances," Grace said with a laugh.

Boone laughed as well.

She fiddled with the bottom of the sweatshirt he loaned her.

"How did you sleep?" he asked.

Truth be told, the couch wasn't the most comfortable situation she'd ever had. But she'd been warm and more than content, with a roof over her head and the most attractive host a girl could dream of. Which she did.

Not knowing quite how to compile all of that into a sentence, she mustered a simple, "Fine, thanks."

Their conversation was a dead end compared to how green light things were between them the night before. She couldn't grasp what had shifted between them. Did he regret kissing her? Had she embarrassed him by stopping him before things went too far?

The lacy curtains framing both sides of the window were parted, revealing glass that had a slightly distressed appearance along the edges, as though it wasn't completely flat or smooth. This house must really be old.

Grace examined the view and found it breathtaking yet again. Snow spread itself on everything it could, dusting every surface like icing. Icicles dripped from branches like silver thread. The sheer whiteness at every angle hinted at innocence and purity, the sparkling color of magic and untouchable things. It was spectacular.

"It's beautiful outside," Grace said. "No more storm." Interesting, that something so rough and dangerous had resulted in something so lovely and mesmerizing.

"It's cleared enough for me to take you back."

Grace frowned. Boone's voice held no traces of being awe-struck by the snow. In fact, his comment was colder than her bones had been the night before. Where did this come from? She didn't want him to go back to being wintry. She wanted the hot Boone, the one who melted her with a single glance.

"I don't want to head back," she said. At least, not right away. She wanted to enjoy as much time with him as she could.

"I need to take you back, Grace."

She gasped at the little pang of discomfort his admission stabbed into her. This was like a math problem she'd been working on for hours and still hadn't managed to find the correct answer to. His reaction so did not measure up with the contented delight coursing through her moments before. Did he want to be rid of her that badly?

"Are you saying you regret our kiss?" she asked. She didn't want to. She dreaded the answer, but for some reason, she had to know.

Tongs in hand, he frowned at her. "You're direct, aren't you?"

"I have to be," she said. "I can't fly home thinking I did something wrong or took advantage of your hospitality."

"What does that mean?"

She gestured to the window. The view outside was no longer beauty and splendor. Now it was frost and menace. "I'm the reason we're stuck out here because I asked you for a sleigh ride. With emotions high last night, I just don't want you to regret me or think badly of me or something." Because it totally sounded like he did.

Boone removed the skillet from the burner, placing it on a hot pad. He set down the tongs beside it and faced her. His eyes shouted with sadness, with something unspeakable burning in the centers. He had a serious battle going on inside of him, one she didn't fully understand.

"Grace, I don't regret you. I thought about you all night long. You made me feel like I haven't in a long time. That's why I'm trying to keep my distance from you this morning, you beautiful, aggravating woman. I'm trying to be good."

Oh goodness, he gave her a smirk that could melt the snow.

Grace swallowed down a lump in her throat, attempting to grasp his meaning. "Then you don't regret kissing me last night?"

His fists clenched at his sides. He stared at a spot on the floor. "I don't think I've ever had a kiss take me over like that. Not for years. I was about ready to lose myself in your lips and that wouldn't be fair to you."

Her blood heated in her veins. All night long, she'd nestled into the night's happy turn and wondered if he was as enthralled by her as she was by him. But this admission? She'd never expected to hear anything like that. "It wouldn't?" she asked.

"No. Not when I can't promise you more than that. If we're getting that close to each other, it should mean more than a one-time-only kind of thing. You've got a man waiting for you back home. A job, a family. And I'm a recluse here, miles away from anyone else and who spends most of his time with horses. We can't have more than last night, so I don't want to fill either of us with false hope."

His voice carried an edge of agony with it. Was he really worrying about her or himself? She'd told him how unhappy she was back in Arizona. She'd be ready to give it all up if he was offering.

But that was so foolish she couldn't even say it. They'd only just met. He was right; a kiss like what they'd shared last night made it feel like they were more connected than they actually were. She didn't even remember his last name!

Boone had lost someone he loved, and he clearly didn't want to get close to anyone like that again.

"She's why you don't like Christmas, isn't she?" Grace asked softly. "It reminds you of her."

Boone turned back to the bacon. Its scent called to Grace's empty stomach. She held out the plate on the counter, and he placed the strips onto the paper towel situated there, patting atop them with another paper towel to absorb the grease.

"It happened the night before Christmas," he said sadly. "I left everything behind when she died because everything reminds me of her. But Christmas worst of all."

Sorrow strummed in her chest. She couldn't imagine how this made him feel. She'd never had a person close to her pass away, but enduring the loss of someone so close had to be a bombshell. Then to have it happen at such a pivotal time of year? One that kept coming around every December? "I'm so sorry. I can see why this time of year is painful for you."

He may not think so, but loving again after losing someone was possible. While she wasn't so sure about Santa Claus, she fully believed that.

"What if..." she began, pressing on before she lost her nerve. "What if we tried to make this work? I don't know about you, but I'm not ready to let you go." She'd never been this decisive in her life, but she was surer than anything that she wanted to get to know him better. She didn't want last night to be their only kiss.

"Her name was Grace." His voice was whisper-soft.

"What?"

"Amy and I. It was the name we'd picked out for our daughter. All good things come from Christ's grace. We wanted her to have that name. Lovely as you are, I can't have that reminder."

Tears stung her eyes. She remembered how he'd recoiled the day they met. She'd thought his withdrawal was because she claimed not to believe in Santa Claus, but his disgust was because of her. Grace. She read what he wasn't saying. No matter what solutions the two of them tried for, she could never escape her own name.

"Then you never should have kissed me," she said.

His eyes were hard again when they met hers. "You're right. But I won't say I'm sorry for that."

What did that mean?

He didn't explain, and she didn't ask. Instead, he scrambled the eggs and kept their conversation to trivial things like the cost of oats and oils and sleigh repairs, and to Grace's work history and if she'd worked anywhere else besides the call center.

Once the eggs were ready, they ate breakfast in silence, with only the sounds of the fire flickering in the grate. Ordinarily, Grace loved bacon, but she couldn't enjoy its distinct taste. With the way Boone stared at his plate, at the floor, at the wall, everywhere but at her, she suddenly wanted to be anywhere but where he was.

One article at a time, both Grace and Boone armored up in their snow garb. Grace changed back into her regular clothes, now dry and a little stiff from being near the fire. She stuffed her feet back into her thin boots.

The morning air was even chillier than it had been the night before. Sunlight made the snow blinding, but the forest view was a wonder to behold. Everything seemed so fragile, so breakable, being covered in whiteness as it was. The sun left a sparkle everywhere it touched. The sight helped to lift her momentary woes, and she found herself smiling.

"This is so gorgeous," she said, holding out her hands as if to catch the twinkle in her fingers. "This is amazing. Do you ever step outside and just stare at what you have here?"

"I don't know. I guess I see it all the time so it's not that amazing to me."

She whacked his arm. "Then stop and look. Look!"

Boone stood with her and inhaled, gazing around at the trees.

Something shifted inside of him. A thought crossed his expression. He lowered the bridle and inhaled, gazing around at the trees. They shared the moment together, letting go of the urgency to leave and just *look* instead.

Grace inhaled, swallowing as much of the brisk morning air as she could. "I adore snow. There, I said it."

His brow furrowed. "Are you not supposed to say it?"

She rubbed a hand on her arm. "Not according to my dad. He can't stand the cold and I get that, but how could anyone hate a view like this? And you have all of this right here, in your palm."

Before she knew what was happening, something struck her hard in the shoulder.

Grace reacted, leaping with a little shriek. She peered down to find a splat of snow on her coat. Grinning incredulously, she searched him out, only to dodge Boone's second snowball just in time.

"What are you doing?" she asked, bracing her hands over her head.

"Snow isn't that amazing," he said, patting another snowball together and lobbing it in her direction.

"That's it," Grace said, shrieking with laughter and diving for a snowball of her own. She was struck more often than she hit him, but by the time their fight ended, she'd gotten close enough for him to capture her in his arms. And in a swift motion of surprising and impressive strength, Boone lifted her and tossed her to the ground on a pile of soft snow.

Grace's laughter reached the treetops. She fought him, squealing away as he tried to stuff snow down her back. "Come on! You know how much the cold affects me."

"Then I'll just have to heat you up again, won't I?" The statement sent a hot streak of awareness up her spine.

Grace brushed it off as quickly as she could. "What happened to 'I need to take you back?'" She grabbed a handful of snow and tossed it in his face. Boone shook off the snow's white traces, snarled, and bowled into her, wrestling with her so the tracks they left behind as they rolled didn't resemble snow angels so much as boulders.

They lay there, side by side, catching their breath and staring upward at the length of the pine trees spearing into the sky. It was amazing to Grace that even though every bough was iced with snow-like frosting, the weight of that snow couldn't force the branches down. They remained outward, holding their shape as if they had an idea of the exquisite sight they offered by doing so.

Cold encompassed the back of her head and neck, but she

rested her hands on her chest and took in the view. Neither of them spoke. They were both lost in their thoughts, and the longer they lay there, not speaking, the more Grace wondered what was going through Boone's mind. He'd said he was trying to keep his distance from her. But what was that comment about wanting to warm her up again?

She couldn't go there. He was right—today was Christmas Eve and she was leaving as soon as the pass opened. She had to arrange a new flight and would be on the next available one back to a world of heated desert air and confined work conditions. It was better they not explore the prospect again.

Grace rose to her knees and brushed her once-again wet gloves over her jeans. "Snow is literally seeping into my clothes," she said.

"It does that."

She punched him gently. "Then why did you tackle me and force it down my shirt?"

Boone's smile could stop traffic. That dimple could have something to do with its effect over her. He pushed himself to his elbows. "You were going on and on about how much you loved it. I wanted to see if you'd still love it once you saw its bad side."

She brushed away more snow, trying to figure out the best place to put her hands to stand. Probably somewhere she'd already matted down instead of a fresh spot. "You're impossible."

He shrugged and stood without the same concerns. "I am on the naughty list, remember?"

"You are now. And you're especially on mine."

Only one of his brows rose. "Am I? All right then. I'd hate to give you the impression that I was good all the time."

"Aren't you?"

"Not all the time. Where's the fun in that?" He winked at her and offered her a hand. She took it, but instead of letting him help her to her feet, she yanked hard, forcing him to crash down beside her instead. He landed closer to her than she'd anticipated, and their coats made a swishing sound at the impact.

"What was that?" he demanded with half incredulity and half delight.

"What?" she said, attempting an innocent look. "I never said *I* was on the nice list."

"I'll show you the nice list," he grumbled, bowling into her again. Grace laughed, trying for all she was worth to get him back and stuff snow down the back of *his* shirt. But he was too swift. He threw his weight and captured her arms, pinning her to the cold ground.

"Hey!" she said with another laugh. "That's not fair."

"It's totally fair," he said, rising just enough. She expected him to move away, but he settled there, smiling at her, looking more alive and happier than Grace had yet seen him.

A mutual realization passed between them. Boone backed away, while his hands supported her to sit up. He removed his snowy glove and skimmed her jaw with surprisingly warm fingers.

"I was wrong," he said.

"About what?"

"I shouldn't take you back. I should keep you here with me."

"I believe that would be called kidnapping."

"Not if you wanted to stay too. Didn't you say you wanted to stay?"

Grace was at a loss for words. "That's a romantic notion," she said.

"But?"

She exhaled and watched her breath puff in the cold air before fading away. "But you were right. I'm leaving. We need to let this...whatever it is...go."

"After I do this," he said. He guided her face to his, and she didn't stop him. His lips were cold, and yet this snow kiss was her favorite one they'd shared. It tasted like sunshine and secret things. She got the sense of how light felt when it passed through an icicle at just the right angle, how it refracted and broke into a thousand beams of color. His kiss made her feel like that beam, brought to life and made so much more than she could be on her own.

And then, just like that, the colors faded. Coldness returned as he pulled away, and she knew she couldn't keep him. Much as she wanted to, this could never be what they both wanted it to be. She really did have a plane to catch.

His reservations earlier that morning didn't leave her alone either. Though he was acting so different now, she wondered if he was only trying to soak up as much of her company as he could before she left.

This time, she let him help her up. Together, Grace and Boone trudged a path to the sleigh and unburied as much snow as they could. She swiped snow free from the bench and scooped it out of the sleigh while Boone fed and prepped Hazelnut. And then, silently, they sat. Boone clicked his teeth and guided Hazelnut back to the inn.

Their conversation during breakfast tormented her the entire way. Grace couldn't appreciate the splendor of the snow-capped trees. Cold soaked into her bones once more, chasing away the last dregs of Boone's warmth. She would go back home once the pass opened. And try as she might, she would never forget the way a cowboy from Montana had kissed her.

16

G race's shower lasted much longer than it should have. If she'd been at home, her mom would have been pounding on the door, demanding she shut the water off and save some for everyone else. But she wasn't at home. She was at an inn in northern Montana and had just had the most incredible, heartrending night of her life.

Boone's presence had imprinted on the underside of her skin. She saw his face every time she closed her eyes. She heard his voice in between sprays of water. And she hugged herself, remembering how entrancing being held by him had felt. He'd started out as gruff, and now she fully understood why. He kept himself closed off from people on purpose. A person who'd been burned so badly before would rarely put himself that close to a fire ever again.

That made the fact that he'd opened up to Grace that much more impactful. He'd tried keeping his distance from her. He'd been brusque and impersonal at times, and yet even on the sleigh ride before the snow went berserk, he'd talked to her. Things only progressed from there, going to unbelievable levels. Kissing by the fireplace. Hearing about his past, about his heartbreak, and discovering the secrets he kept buried so deeply inside.

She couldn't blame him for pulling back again. That didn't mean knowing why made it any easier. He'd said she was the first woman after his wife he'd ever gotten close to. He'd called her both beautiful and aggravating, in such an endearing way. That had to mean something, didn't it? She couldn't believe he would continue to stay away from her after that, yet they both agreed they would.

When he'd dropped her off, he hadn't kissed her. That kiss during their play in the snow was the last one she knew she'd ever receive from him. He'd said goodbye and guided Hazelnut on to the barn. Shortly afterward, she noticed him riding the horse back into the forest without a sleigh.

Unwittingly, other conversations began in her mind as she stood there, letting the shower's warmth and humidity enshroud her—conversations between her fictional characters she'd been trying to tap into for days now.

She wasn't sure whether it was the effect of the hot water on her muscles, or the way the relaxing prickles began at the top of her skull and traveled their way down her spine to the backs of her heels, but showering always loosened ideas and thoughts in her mind. So many times she'd gotten stuck in a manuscript, unsure of where to take the story or what to do next, when during an unsuspecting shower, the solution became clear.

This was both awesome and frustrating, because it wasn't like she had paper and pen in the shower. If there was anything she learned since becoming a writer, it was that once an idea struck, if she didn't write it down, it wouldn't last long.

This was a similarly heart wrenching scene between the heroine and her hero, a gripping, emotional conversation where both characters laid their hearts out for the other to see after keeping their feelings to themselves for so long. It was going to be a pivotal moment in her book, one to keep readers enthralled on the edges of their seats, she just knew it.

Grace hurriedly washed her hair, clutching onto the characters' dialogues rambling in her mind. She turned the water off, dried as quickly as she could, and knotted the towel around herself. Her crocheted bag slumped on the floor by the bed, right where she'd plopped it down when she came back in. She grasped for it.

The bag wasn't as heavy as usual. Ignoring this, Grace dove a hand in, ready for the notebook that always sat inside—the one she'd taken during her sleigh ride, the one she'd stuffed in the bag when the snow had picked up so quickly the day before.

But the more she dug for the notebook, the less she found it. Her hand swept one direction, then the other, only to come up with a few empty gum wrappers and one of her pens.

"Oh no," she breathed. Memory flooded her brain as she attempted to retrace her steps. All notions of retrieving the notebook had been forgotten just being around Boone. Had she left the notebook at his cottage? Where did it go? She worried it had fallen out of the sleigh while they'd been playing in the snow. Or maybe she'd lost it along the way home, though she didn't think she'd taken it out at all during the return trip. *Had* she lost it along the way?

Or worst of all—was it still at his cottage?

"No, no, no," she said, placing a hand on the knot keeping her towel in place. Panic pushed her to her feet with nowhere to go. She'd written more than just her stories in that notebook. After he'd kissed her, and before drifting off to sleep, she'd poured a soap-opera episode's worth of romantic, stupid feelings in there, things no one else was ever meant to read, least of all the man she'd written them about.

Last night Boone asked if he could read what she was writing. Was he the kind of man who would peek without permission? Hopefully, he wasn't the kind of man who would invade her written privacy, even if she was fool enough to leave the notebook behind.

"It'll be fine," she told herself. She didn't have his number. She didn't have a clue how to get back to his cottage, but she did know where the barn was. "I'll just head out to the barn. Find him there."

But that wasn't right. He hadn't stayed. This was Christmas Eve. He'd headed back to the cottage once he dropped her and the sleigh off.

There had to be some way to reach him. Grace dressed quickly but with care. She picked her favorite shirt with the vintage red truck on the front and a pine tree in its truck bed. She tucked her skinny jeans into her knee length boots and dusted makeup onto her face. He'd seen her wake up—but she still wanted to make a good impression, considering how he'd all but ended things between them the last time they'd spoken.

They'd agreed to let things between them go. She could make it clear she only wanted the notebook, couldn't she? Ugh, not if this ridiculous excitement at the prospect of seeing him again kept up. She'd never been able to hide her feelings. Undoubtedly, she wouldn't be able to hide from him how much she wanted to be near him again once she was, well, near him.

"It'll be fine," she told herself, pausing at her room's door and keeping her hand on the handle. "We'll keep our distance. I'm going home. I have to remember that."

Voices resonated in the hall the minute she stepped into it. The same woman Grace had spoken with the night she'd heard the radio play was out in the hall again, but she wasn't alone this time. Her auburn hair was in a bun on top of her head, and rather than the friendly smile she'd offered Grace the other night, agitation showed clearly on her pretty face. She faced a handsome man standing at the other end of the hall and called out, "No, I'm not, because it's not *my* room, remember?"

The man raised a finger to his lips to shush her and hurried toward the woman. "People are going to think we're nuts, Lacie," he said. "Will you please calm down?"

The woman folded her arms. "Jared," she said with exasperation, "I want to go home."

"Everything okay?" Grace asked. She had the feeling she'd stepped right into a couple's squabble, but since she was already in the middle of it, she couldn't exactly pretend like she hadn't heard what they were shouting, especially not when she and the woman—Lacie—had chatted in such a friendly way before.

"No, it's not okay," Lacie said, folding her arms and turning to Grace. "Since the minute we got to this inn, our lives have turned upside down. No one will believe we're not married. Even the computers are showing my last name is something it isn't!"

Jared rolled his eyes and closed the rest of the distance between him and the two women. Grace didn't know what to say.

"I had my own room when we first got here. Now it's gone and I can't even go home because all this snow closed the pass. So we're stuck here. Sharing a room together." She flapped a hand in Jared's direction.

Grace still didn't quite grasp everything she was saying, not without knowing the nature of their relationship to one another. How could Lacie have a room of her own before and not now? "What—"

Lacie pressed a hand to her forehead. "Forget it. But if you hear music from the fancy radio downstairs? Run."

This warning pricked Grace like the time she'd stuck her tongue on the end of a battery just to see what would happen. A jolt of power stronger than she'd anticipated zinged right into her.

Lacie attempted to open the door next to her, but Grace stuck out a hand. "Sorry, but what do you mean? The radio downstairs? Do you mean the one they claim was delivered here by Santa Claus himself?"

Conflict rested in Lacie's gaze, striking pity within Grace. Whatever was happening to these two, it clearly distressed them both. Had they heard the radio play too?

"I mean that thing is wreaking havoc on our lives," Lacie said, lowering her voice this time. "I've been snowed in here with my best friend." She gestured to Jared, who gave Grace a casual wave. "We were married by a snowman, and now whatever supposed *magic*," she bent the first two fingers on each of her hands, "is streaming from that radio, it's completely messing things up!"

"Hang on," Grace said. "You mean you were married *next to* a snowman?"

Lacie peered behind her. Jared gave her an it's-up-to-you kind of shrug, and she moved in, lowering her voice. "No. We were married *by* snowman. I mean, a snowman pronounced us husband and wife. You know, like the song." She bobbed her head a little as if to lighten the impact of her words.

Grace's eyebrows shot upward. "You—a snowman married you two?" She wasn't sure what to say. Was Lacie serious?

"Yeah. I know it sounds insane, but we were building a snowman outside and then we heard this music and the snowman like, spoke. I asked that girl, Junie, the one at the desk, you know? And she admitted they have this joke in their family that the radio is some kind of matchmaker."

"Junie said that?" Did Boone think the same thing? Was that why he'd gotten so angry at the radio that day?

Lacie went on. "Once that pass opens, we're going home, but

I'm not even sure that will do anything. Will everyone there think we're married too? Are we going to have to get some kind of divorce now? I mean, he has a girlfriend who was so not happy he'd come here with me at all in the first place. We can't possibly be *married* if he has feelings for someone else."

Grace had a difficult time keeping up with Lacie's ramblings. "So...you came here together. As friends. You heard the radio play and now everyone thinks you're married?"

"Yes!" Lacie and Jared both exclaimed at once.

Whoa. Talk about intervention. Grace swallowed, attempting to figure out where to go next. "Does that mean you don't want to be married? Do you want to divorce him? Your...non-husband?"

Jared gazed at Lacie in expectation. A sort of fear lingered behind his gaze, as though he wasn't sure he wanted the answer to this, which didn't make any sense if what Lacie claimed was true and he had a girlfriend waiting for him wherever they were from. Grace felt a smidgeon of guilt for interfering, but she'd sort of been roped into their argument. The least she could do was help if she could.

"No! Yes. I mean, I don't know. I'm seriously confused." Lacie covered her face with her hands. She paced away, with Jared following after before Grace had the chance to ask him another question that was probably too nosy. Did he want his girlfriend, or did he want to stay married to Lacie?

"None of your business, Grace," she muttered to herself, shaking the question away. It was better not to go there. Those two would have to sort that much out themselves. In any case, the other claim in their story was unsettling—the claim that the music from the radio downstairs was the cause of all this confusion.

She and Boone had both heard the radio play too. She'd heard chiming several times as well, once before she'd found the necklace that had made him so angry, and again right before the snow had blasted in seemingly out of nowhere.

Grace's heart stopped in her chest at that last thought. Impulsively, she dashed forward and caught Lacie and Jared on their way to the stairs. "Hang on a second," she said, slightly breathless. The two paused. Lacie gripped the banister and glanced up at Grace.

"Are you saying you think there's something magical going on at this inn?" Grace asked. Boone claimed to believe in Santa Claus. Did that mean he also believed in magic? Not just jokingly in response to her questions, as she'd thought before. But honestly, truly. Magic. Did it really exist? She wrote fantasy, but that didn't mean she thought magic was real.

The chemistry sizzling between the glance Lacie and Jared exchanged was palpable. Much as they tried to deny it, there was something more than friendship going on between these two. No wonder no one would believe they weren't married.

"Yeah," Lacie said. "I mean, a snowman pronounced us man and wife. What else could it be?"

Grace blinked a few times at that. Did Boone know? He had to. He was the one who told Grace about the radio's origins in the first place. Now, more than ever, she needed to talk to him again.

"Come on," Jared said. "We've got to get going before the bonfire tonight."

"What bonfire?" Grace asked, glad for a topic she could wrap her head around.

"It's a Christmas Eve tradition here. The guests pile into the sleighs and ride up the mountain, to the actual point they claim is America's North Pole. There, they tell the story of the night Santa Claus stopped by, and everyone drinks cocoa and sings 'Kumbaya.'"

"Sleigh rides?" Grace took heart at that. She would try the

barn, but if Boone wasn't there, she couldn't exactly go back to his cottage. But from the sound of things, he would be one of the driver's that night. And hopefully, if things went according to plan, she could talk to him about her notebook on the way there.

17

Boone waited until Grace made it inside the inn before climbing back into the sleigh. On principle, he avoided the inn on Christmas Eve. He then drove the sleigh to the barn, unharnessed it, and mounted Hazelnut to ride her back.

Morty, the replacement driver for tonight's bonfire, was here to drive the sleigh. Boone double checked with Troy, and fortunately, Morty had made his way here before the snow had struck. They were all set to drive the sleighs for customers to the inn's annual bonfire for those guests who opted to stay during the holidays. Which meant Boone was free to head back to the cottage.

The sights around him seemed newer, somehow. As though he was seeing snow for the first time, which was ridiculous, because he'd seen it every year of his life. But he couldn't help hearing Grace's admiration for it with every glance. She was right—this scenery really was beautiful.

"Boone!" Junie ran out as he passed the front of the inn on horseback. Her hands splayed in the air as though she'd just finished one of those cheerleader spread-eagle moves. "I knew you wouldn't let me down."

He pressed his eyes closed. Two more minutes. If he'd only left two minutes earlier, he could have avoided this. "I'm not here to help."

Junie hugged her arms around her chest. She was outside without a coat. Air puffed out of her mouth with every breath. "Come on. Please? I need you."

"No, you don't. I was just in the barn. I talked to Troy, and the replacement driver made it here before the pass closed. You're all set."

"Then come with us. You haven't come since you first started working here."

Her plea struck him, but not enough to make him change his mind. He'd sworn off everything Christmas. Being around the guests, hearing them sing Christmas carols while Junie and her mother retold the story of Santa's visit to Harper's. He couldn't. Junie had to know how high on the list his couldn't was.

"I can't be here, Junie. I'm sorry. You know I can't." It was too hard. Boone had made it a point to avoid the inn on Christmas Eve. Just delivering Grace back had unraveled him. He felt his careful composure slipping the longer he lingered.

Junie released a heavy breath, emitting more smoky air from her mouth. Her features sagged along with her shoulders. "I'm sorry, you're right. I should never have asked."

Could he make an exception? Grace had given him a new perspective—and a handful of times he thought he could move on and find happiness again—undoubtedly giving Grace mixed signals in the process. But Boone's fears that he might forget Amy, the way she smiled, the way she smelled, the way she'd looked at him like he was her reason for existence—he couldn't go on, pretending like her loss on such an epic day like Christmas Eve was something that didn't affect him anymore.

It seemed a violation of his love for her, somehow. Celebrating with others meant he'd accepted that Amy was gone. And that was something he could never do.

He knew pushing Grace away had hurt and confused her but loving someone else just wasn't a possibility. She had to know that. That was another reason he had to stay away until she left.

Ugh. If only he could just skip the next few days. He tried it every year, and every year those days passed with painful slowness. This was when he usually readied his home with necessary repairs that he didn't take time for otherwise.

He hesitated only a moment before clicking his teeth. Hazelnut's ears pricked, and he called out. "On, on," he said, giving the horse her usual cues. Hazelnut responded, carrying him back through the woods.

The cottage looked the way it always had, with its familiar, multi-colored stacked stones held together by mortar. Ravaging winds often wore on the exterior and, considering how the place was built sometime in the late eighteen hundreds, it had its fair share of wear and tear.

Every year Boone had to fix cracks in the mortar and the walls, along with roof repairs. He'd had the roof replaced shortly after moving in here, but the passing years had chipped away here and there, not to mention the mice and other small creatures often burrowing in whatever cracks they could find.

Christmas was the perfect time to deal with these repairs. Boone thrived on the sense of purpose this brought. He poured every ounce of energy and mental thought into the jobs, doing his best to avoid looking at the fireplace. Or the couch. Or his bed. Or anywhere else Grace had brightened with her presence.

He retrieved his tool belt and spent the afternoon in the bathroom, mending the leaky pipes beneath the sink. Boone worked with purpose, drowning in his non-Christmas rock music with its heavy beats and angry tones. He lost himself in the work, allowing his mind to get caught up in the lyrics and pushing aside thoughts of Grace, Amy, and Christmas altogether.

Kneeling on the floor, Boone rested a hand against the sink and checked the newly installed u-shaped p-trap pipe. He was grateful the rancid sewer smell he'd dealt with last year hadn't made an appearance while Grace was here.

He shook his head. He wasn't supposed to be thinking of her.

Boone returned the cleaners and sponges to their places beneath the sink. He cleaned up the mess he'd made, returned his tools to their spots in the closet, and took a restful shower.

Time was crawling by. By the time he finished dressing, it wasn't even sunset. Boone shuffled through his living room, deciding to cook some dinner, when something caught his eye.

On the table in his kitchen, Grace's notebook lay splayed open.

Boone frowned and fought the chills speckling along his arms. He veered toward the table, glancing around for a sign of her bright blue, floppy knitted bag. Did she leave her bag here?

"How else did this get left here?" he mused aloud.

In spite of himself, he reflected on the words they'd shared on the couch last night. He'd been curious about her writing since the sleigh ride, and her outright refusal to let him read anything only piqued that curiosity even more.

He really had no intention of reading it, but when he reached to close the book, the words in her delicate cursive scrawl jumped off the page, catching his attention. Or rather, one word stood out, leaping from all the rest as surely as if someone highlighted it.

His second attempt at resistance was as feeble as one-ply toilet paper.

"What the heck," Boone said, giving in, sitting at the table and sliding the notebook close. Grace had made it clear she didn't want him reading her writing, but he couldn't stop now.

I think I just want this...whatever it is between us...to mean something. When he looks at me, it's like our gazes connect. It's an unspoken invitation, and all I want is to be wherever he is.

Boone's knees weakened, threatening to buckle beneath him. "She said she wrote fantasy," he said breathily. "Not reality." If that was the case, what did this mean? Why was she writing about him?

No wonder she didn't want to let him read what she'd been scribbling away about. When had she written this? He flipped through. No date was listed, but she'd written a handful of pages beyond this about a character named Swiftheart Treeborne with pointed ears that pricked at the sound of branches rustling. She had pretty descriptions about snow and trees and the elf's burly, muscular physique that made Boone raise his brows, impressed at her talent in spite of its tendency to gush.

But he flipped back to that excerpt and devoured every word. Over and over, he read her descriptions of himself, of how he made her feel. And those words were like sugar to his bloodstream. They made him crave more.

But he didn't want to read them on a page. He wanted to hear her say them.

Boone slammed the notebook shut at the realization and pushed away from the table so hard he knocked the chair to the floor. Impulsively, he ran both hands through his hair and stared at the book's leather binding.

"What is happening?" he said.

So much of this didn't make sense, and yet he couldn't accept that. What were the chances that this notebook flipped open to this page? He was pretty sure he'd passed his table after getting Hazelnut secured in the barn when he'd first returned, and it wasn't there then.

"The radio," he grumbled under his breath. It had to be. He wasn't exactly sure how the magic worked. All he knew was that in the past, the music had managed to turn people's lives upside down just to get them together. How else could he explain this?

Boone shook his head and laughed, a cold, merciless sound to his own ears. "I'm such a fool," he said, righting the chair once more. "Did she even write this?" he called, raising his voice so Santa—or whoever was apparently watching him and coordinating these events—could hear.

She'd written of magic and being overtaken by his presence. What else was this but getting swept into the music's mischief? "My point exactly," he went on, answering himself. This wasn't real.

His gaze drifted to her notebook again, and he heaved a sigh. Boone retrieved his coat and gloves, then stuffed his feet into his thick boots. "Whether it's real or not," he mumbled, "she'll still need her notebook." He wasn't heartless enough to keep it. This notebook was her key to writing her breakout bestseller. The least he could do was return it.

He tried to quell the jittery excitement the prospect of seeing her again brought with it. He was just returning the notebook. Nothing more.

There could never be anything more.

18

Grace was starting to get frantic. She'd scoured every inch she could think of in the inn, but her notebook was nowhere in sight. Why did time always seem to pass slower when it was being watched?

Would Boone even be coming back for the sleigh ride tonight? She'd kept watch out her window as well, but there had been no further signs of him. What was she going to do if he didn't return?

She'd have to let the notebook go, she guessed. Some of her friends had computers crash or flash drives burn out. They'd lost entire manuscripts. At least she wasn't losing her whole book. She could recapture the thoughts she'd written about the inn, if she really had to.

Though she'd rather not have to.

Guests were gathered along the stairs and in the living room below, peering out the windows. Every person was bundled up in preparation for the sunset ride to wherever this bonfire was slated to be held.

With Grace's beanie snug on her blonde hair, she was starting to cook in all the extra layers she'd put on. She didn't want to miss the bonfire, but considering how cold had taken over her the last time she'd been out in it for an extended period of time, she decided to take a few more precautions and layer up.

"Here they come!" a woman called out, moving from her position at the window and turning to make the pronouncement. Other guests cheered in response. Grace's heart skipped a beat. Sure enough, two large sleighs pulled forward on the snow outside with a pair of horses harnessed to each, waiting for the guests to pile out.

She hurried the rest of the way down the stairs, eager, hoping for a sight of Boone in his thick coat with the wool lining, his tufted fur hat and thick gloves. She passed Lacie and Jared, who were arguing about something near the Christmas tree, and pushed her way out into the night.

Stars speckled, filling the sky overhead and drawing a gasp from her. There was something to be said about the winter sky and the sheer number of stars spoking through. Grace shivered and moved aside for a couple who had followed out after her, only to stop short.

Two men had driven the sleighs, but neither of them was Boone. Her heart sank.

"That's our call!" Junie announced. "Those who are coming for the bonfire, the time to leave is now. I repeat, the sleighs are leaving now!"

People shouted, one woman squealed in excitement, and Grace even noticed the woman who'd been holding the dog now walking hand-in-hand with her daughter toward the sleigh in the front.

Grace hurried to catch Junie's arm. "Junie," she said. "Sorry," she added at the look on surprise on Junie's face. Junie wore a bright pink hat with yarn that seemed to have exploded on her head. It stuck out at all angles but was so endearing on her childish, freckled face that Grace suspected the hat had been designed that way on purpose. And it totally fit Junie's laid-back, spunky style.

"Grace!" she said, her smile wide, breath leaking out in the cold air. "Do you need something? You're joining us, right?"

Junie peered behind her and caught sight of the radio on the table through the window. Grace peered back as well. She was momentarily side-tracked. Boone had stormed off with it; how had the radio gotten back where it was? Considering the perplexed expression on Junie's face, she was wondering the same thing. Grace decided not to ask.

"Have you seen Boone?" Grace asked instead.

Junie's face fell into an apologetic grimace. A good-looking man with dark brows and an eager expression standing beside the sleigh waved to her, and Junie gave him an impatient wave back as if telling him to wait. "Sorry, no, and you probably won't either. Not until after Christmas."

Grace attempted to hide her disappointment. "Oh?"

Junie slipped her hands into a pair of thick, knitted gloves with white reindeer on the back. They were the kind of gloves that folded open to allow her fingertips to poke out. "Yeah, he sort of goes into hiding." Another grimace.

Grace glanced at the crowds. The only reason she'd been ready to brave another night of cold was the possibility of being with Boone again. No amount of submersion into a winter night would be worth the torturous cold in her bones tonight. She may be without her notebook, but she could still type on her laptop. She'd be better off staying at the inn if Boone wasn't among the crowd.

But she still needed to talk to him before she left tomorrow. Rumor was, the pass was being cleared. The road would be clear enough for her to summon an Uber driver and make her way to the small airport in West Hills. The airport was rescheduling flights. Tomorrow was Christmas, and she was leaving. She couldn't without seeing him one more time.

"Does he have a cell phone or some way I can call him? I really need to talk to him."

The man down by the sleigh waved Junie forward, a little more exuberantly this time. Grace thought she recognized him as the inn's chef, but she couldn't quite tell. She hadn't exactly gotten a good look at him, considering how most of her meals had been spent in her room or with Boone.

Junie called for him to hang on. "I'll be right there!" she said before turning back to Grace. "Don't take this the wrong way, but our policy is not to give out personal contact information to guests—and believe me, a lot of women ask for his."

This comment made Grace squirm. He'd said she was the first woman he allowed himself to touch since he lost his wife. The thought made Junie's remark even more striking. Whatever expression was on Grace's face, it drew out a sympathetic pout from Junie.

"I'm really sorry," the receptionist said. "I wish I could make an exception, but I can't do that without getting his permission first."

"I understand," Grace said, disappointed. And she really did. She'd want the same discretion from one of her managers at the office if a random person came asking for her personal contact information.

"Let's get this show on the road!" the chef called again. Others among the guests cheered and shouted their agreement, waving to her.

"Come on, Junie! Let's go!" someone cried.

"I'm coming!" she replied, smiling. Excitement beamed in her eyes, rivaling the moonlight spearing down at them. To her credit, Junie didn't abandon Grace immediately. She gripped Grace by the elbows. "Are you sure you won't come? It's going to be amazing. Cold, but the fire combats that. We serve cocoa up there and everything."

Grace backed away with a sniff—from the frosty air, not her emotions. At least, that was what she told herself. "I'm okay. I think I'll check out the hot tub." And get some more words in.

She had to accept it. Boone had told her goodbye, and he'd meant it. She was leaving and she would never see him again.

Head down, she turned when a distinctive rumbling caught her ears. Grace's brow furrowed. She attempted to peer for its source, but the inn's porch stretched across the front of the structure, blocking her view.

Junie, on the other hand, groaned and tossed her hands on the air. "Are you kidding me?" In a huff, she stomped to the end of the porch and peered beyond its corner. "Perfect. Just perfect."

"What is it?" Grace asked. It sounded like some kind of vehicle, but she'd never heard anything like it before.

Junie stormed back toward her, fuming. "What does he think he's doing? Why did he ride that thing up here? He knows the tracks will leave marks on the snow and ruin the setting!"

"Junie, come on!" the chef barked with impatience.

She stormed down the steps and grumbled the entire time. "I'm going to kill him," she said to the chef, accepting his hand and climbing onto the empty space on the sleigh beside him. "Tell him that, will you?" she shouted to Grace as the vehicle sound grew louder. "Tell him I'll kill him for ruining the landscape!"

Grace couldn't help the smile spearing over her cheeks. The two drivers signaled their horses and jiggled the reins. Both teams responded, and jingling bells signaled their advancement on the snow. They traveled along the road, curving up toward the moon and out of sight.

Meanwhile, Grace watched the trees in anxious anticipation. A faint light came into view, and the distinctive *brrraap brraap* noise increased. A snowmobile cleared between two trees, and immediately Grace understood what made Junie so upset. Its tracks ruffled the snow, leaving jagged, linear trails behind. That didn't really fit in with the cozy, secluded, back-in-time feel the inn portrayed.

Boone slowed the lime green snowmobile feet from her, letting it rumble. A distinguishable smell of exhaust spewed from the vehicle, taking over the air around her. Grace waved it away, coughing a few times.

To her relief, Boone shut off the ignition. The resulting quiet was a contrast to the snowmobile's loud rumble. He lifted one leg and dismounted—if that was the right word. Grace couldn't be sure. Still, she took in his every movement, from the sure way he carried himself to how he lifted his arms to remove his helmet and tuck it beneath one arm.

Be still her beating heart. His hair was deliciously rumpled, and his glorious face stole the spotlight from the stars.

"Grace," he said.

"What are you doing here?" she asked, glancing at his machine once more. "And why...on a snowmobile?" She couldn't help wondering why he hadn't busted this thing out during the storm. Where did he keep it? She hadn't seen it in his barn. Then again, she hadn't been looking for it.

He must have heard her unspoken question. "I know what you're thinking, but I couldn't have used this the other night to take you back. It wouldn't have been safe to take out in that blizzard, not with how low visibility was. Some models come equipped with GPS, but even then, in a storm you still chance hitting a tree or falling into a crevice because you can't see."

"Right," she said, so grateful that was the case, because she wouldn't have traded her snowed-in night with Boone for anything. A smirk found its way to her face. She stepped forward and rested a hand on the snowmobile's handle. "You know, Junie said she's going to kill you for this."

He dipped his head to hide his smile, but she still saw the dimple peek through. "I know. She and her mother have given very specific instructions about my snowmobile, but they know it's an emergency-machine-only."

"And this was an emergency?" Junie hadn't seemed to think so.

His gaze turned solemn and serious. He tucked in his lower lips just enough. "I had to see you before you left."

She reached for the words, waiting for something to land on her tongue, to give voice to the flutter in her chest, but nothing of any definition in any kind of verbal language came forward. She spoke his name, then. Only his name.

"Boone," she said.

Gravity was in his gaze. That look was a force all its own, one that connected with the part of her soul that was destined to be with his. She was aware of everything in that moment. The erratic rhythm of her heartbeat. The sweat collecting in her palms. The moonlight shining down on the frosty snow. And the pull emanating from Boone to be as close to him as possible.

Boone cleared his throat, breaking the connection in their gazes long enough for her to scratch out a breath. "To give you this, I mean," he corrected. He turned his back to her and retrieved something in his saddlebag. There had to be a different name besides 'saddlebag' for the leather pouch situated beneath his snowmobile seat, since he wasn't riding on a saddle, but she wasn't exactly up to speed on snowmobile terminology.

In any case, he closed its flap, securing the snaps, and faced her once more with a familiar notebook in his hand and a smirk on his lips.

"Oh my gosh," Grace said, pulling her hands to her chest. Her breath left in small puffs of air. "You did have it!"

"It was sitting on my dining table," he said. "I know how important it is to you. You probably wouldn't want to leave without it."

Grace's elation faded, replaced by confusion. Once again, she wasn't sure what to say. How had the notebook made its way to his table when she had been careful to make sure it made its way back into her bag?

Unless...

She didn't want to think it. He hadn't come rummaging through her bag when she'd gone to bed or something, had he? Would he do that? The thought was ludicrous, but she had to voice it.

"Did you take it from my bag?" she asked.

He gripped the notebook with both hands this time. "I didn't. I swear. It was just sitting there."

She fought down a wedge in her throat. "And did you...read it?"

He contemplated his answer for several seconds. His gaze roamed over her. "You look cold," he said in that way he had of not answering her questions.

"I am. But you aren't going to distract me from this question. Did you read my notebook?"

"Let's go inside."

"Boone."

He placed the helmet on the snowmobile's dark seat and stepped closer. "I will tell you the answer to that because I think we should talk. But I don't think we should do it out here. Okay?"

Sure enough, Grace's jaw was starting to judder again. Man, was she glad she hadn't gone on the sleigh ride to the bonfire. Snow was pretty enough to look at, but extended time in its company was asking too much of her. Then again, getting frost-bite could incite another snuggle session...

With equal parts reservation and anticipated excitement, she nodded. "Okay."

Boone walked her up the stairs. He smelled like snowmobile exhaust and exhilaration. He tossed his head to the side and reached for the inn's door first, holding it so Grace could step through.

The heat was a welcome friend. She was ready to nestle in near the fire and stay a good long while. The room's only glow came from the fire beneath the mantel and the pinches of light glittering on the Christmas tree, but it was more than enough. Grace scurried close to the fire, hands at the ready for warmth. Boone removed his coat and placed it on one of the coat rack's vacant arms before following her into the front room.

Grace noticed he didn't once glance at the Christmas tree. She took her coat off but left her beanie on. The fire's warmth helped thaw out the parts that had gotten cold outside. She settled into the squashy armchair beside the fire while Boone paced back and forth along the carpet in front of the radio.

"This is dangerous territory," she said, quirking a brow at the radio and his reaction to its proximity. "Are you sure you want to be in here?"

"Is there somewhere else you'd rather go?"

Grace thought it over. "You said you grew up here in this inn?"

"I did."

She held her hands in front of her. "Where at?"

He stared at her for so long she wondered if he was going to speak. Then, after winning whatever mental battle was going on, he nodded. "All right then. But don't ever tell Junie I took you."

19

G race couldn't help the giggle that erupted as she followed him. She felt so sneaky, so discreet. To her surprise—and relief—Boone took her hand in his and led her toward the dining room. To the left was the spa section of the inn that Grace had yet to visit. To the right was the corridor Boone had stormed down when he'd taken the radio from the front room the day they'd heard it play.

"Everything else was remodeled but this section," he said. "This was my parents' room." He pointed to the door on the right. "Junie's is here."

"Is?"

"Yep, she's had the same room her whole life. And her mom's is here." He pointed to the next one. "And then this..." He dug a set of keys from his pocket. They jangled in his hand, and he selected a slim key, turning to insert it into the lock. "This was my room."

He opened the door and waited for Grace to enter before clicking on the lamp situated on the dresser by the door. Her heart lodged itself in her throat. This was what she'd hoped to see of him back at his cottage. A calendar from 2005 hung on the wall featuring pictures of horses. Prize ribbons created a montage of color above a narrow bed with an old bedspread, rustic and covered in horseshoe fabric. Several cowboy hats hung from pegs on the wall and a poster labeled as the *Roadkill Café,* with all kinds of gruesome offerings, hung.

It was tidy and clean. And she had a better idea of teenage Boone than she would have if he'd just told her some of these things.

"It looks like sixteen-year-old you will be back any minute."

He pulled at his neck and leaned against the dresser by the closet. "Yeah, that was my mom. She wanted me to have a place of my own if I ever needed it."

"Then why didn't you move back here when you came back?"

He stared at his hands. "They needed someone to keep an eye on that old cottage. Local kids kept breaking into it and trashing things inside. And I wanted solitude." He gave her a sad smile.

She nodded, heart pricking at his words. "I get that." Grace took a few steps farther into the room and rotated, holding out her arms before resting them at her sides again. "All right, we're inside," she said. "Please tell me. Did you read my notebook?" She gestured to it, still in his hands.

"I...saw a page or two."

Her eyes closed.

"Is it true?" His voice was a whisper. It tiptoed to her across the space.

"Is what true?"

He flagged the notebook in the air. "Are these really your feelings? Or am I only going to become a character in your book?"

Grace pinched her nose. She couldn't tell if the prospect bothered him or not. And she wasn't entirely sure what to say.

From the minute she'd met him, he'd gotten under her skin and she couldn't help trying to craft a character after someone so interesting. She wasn't going to go into all of that. "They're true. I kept trying to write but all I could think about was you, and I couldn't concentrate on anything else until I got down how you made me feel—"

"That's all I needed to know." He swooped in and scooped her in his arms. Tight against his chest, it took no effort at all to tilt her face and meet him halfway. His mouth had urgency, a parched sort of thirst for only her. She moved her lips to match his pace, allowing his to part hers, to deepen the taste, the feel, the wanting flourishing inside of her.

Boone kissed her long, slow, and hard, so much so that, when he lowered her until her feet returned to the floor, she had to lean against him for several moments to regain her bearings.

"I've thought about nothing but you since you left," he said, his thumbs stroking her cheeks.

Her smile bloomed. "I thought you couldn't have the reminder of your daughter's name."

"I was trying to convince us both it would never work because you looked so amazing in the just-woke-up kind of way, and it was all I could do not to take you in my arms again and kiss you then and there."

Grace's heart swelled in her chest with relief. Still, there was more he'd mentioned, another reason to keep his distance, and she had to ask. "Were you really going to name your daughter Grace?"

A muscle ticked in his jaw, but he didn't take his chocolate brown eyes from hers. "Yes. But I didn't mean what I said. You aren't a painful reminder. I've been hiding from my heart for so long. I hide away at the cottage until Christmas is over because I can't bear the reminder, but now you're everywhere there too.

"I was going to wait out the holiday, except you left me this love note." He pointed to the notebook, which he'd placed on the dresser behind him.

"I can't believe I've only known you for a matter of days," she said. She pressed her forehead to his. "It feels like I've known you so much longer."

"I know," he said. "I've been trying to figure that out too."

"Please tell me you didn't read the Demon Boone parts of my story."

He laughed and pulled away to look into her eyes. "The what?"

Sheepish, she ducked her head. "Back when I was angry at you, I made you the villain."

Boone laughed harder, pulling her closer to him once more. "I didn't read anything like that." His thumb stroked her jaw and his inquisitive gaze poured into hers. "But I did read how you were confused by my actions."

Oh right. That part.

His brows folded down. "Are you still confused by me, Grace?"

She hooked her hand around his wrist, and he continued to stroke her cheek and gaze into her eyes. "Absolutely. You are a mystery to me. This whole situation, why you'd even want me is a mystery."

"I told you no woman has caught my eye since my wife died. And plenty of them have tried."

"But why? I can't read you. Sometimes you're so open and expressive and I think you're okay with me. And other times you push me away and have this mask, this wall, like you don't want me anywhere near you."

"That's my own inner battle," he said. "That doesn't mean I don't want you. If anything, it means I want you more than I should."

Grace shook her head. "I don't get that."

He rubbed her arms. "I'm not sure how to explain. Letting you into my life...after I've shut everyone out for so long. It's not easy."

"I get that. It's just—"

"Just what? What else confuses you?"

Grace left his embrace, stepped away, needing to think. He'd shown her his past. She could do the same. Keeping her eyes closed, she spoke. "Because I'm so unwantable. Rejection is my lot in life—with my writing, with my love life, with my career. It's why I've been stuck at that stupid job, because every other job I've tried for turned me down. I've just gotten used to it."

"You got rejected?"

"My first book, yeah. I submitted it to agents and none of them wanted it."

Boone leaned his elbows back on the dresser behind him. "Yet you're not giving up on your writing."

"No, I'm not," she said, unsure of where he was going with this.

He stepped away from the dresser and closer to her. "That doesn't sound like a woman who's accepted rejection. Or a woman who is unwantable. It's just some words on a page. It doesn't reflect who you are as a person."

His tender words rang with so much truth they brought tears to her eyes. "Thank you."

"And from what I read, your words aren't the problem."

Her breathing stilled, making her heartbeat that much more noticeable. "How much did you read?"

He inched closer. "Enough to know that you're crazy about me."

She gave him a playful smile. "You mean you couldn't already tell?"

His fingers found hers. Just a touch, but its warmth trailed up her arms. "Then you should know, you're having the same effect on me."

She exhaled sharply. "I am?"

"Yes. That's why I'm having such a hard time staying away from you. Even though I know I should. So, know this, you tantalizing woman, that from what I can see, and taste" —he dipped in for a kiss— "and smell and touch, you are completely wantable."

He couldn't know how his words struck her right in that moment. In one fell swoop, he'd told her everything she didn't know she needed to hear. Tears welled in her eyes at his sincerity, at his admission, at his everything, and she struggled to take a breath.

"I know you're leaving. I know we can never have more than tonight."

"I know," she breathed, inhaling the scent of two-stroke exhaust still embedded into his skin. She loved that smell. That was the smell of impulsive action just to get to her, and it meant so much. More than he could possibly know.

His fingers closed over hers, and they stood there in a motionless dance, bodies barely skimming, breath heating the air between them, foreheads together while dreams and desires of what could never be were shared like unspoken secrets. "They're going to be gone until at least midnight," he said. "So tell me more about you."

She blinked at this and reared back enough to look into the glimmer of his dark eyes. "More about me?"

"Yes." He kissed her again. "I want to know everything."

They settled on his bed with their backs to the wall and their feet dangling over its end. Boone held her hand while they talked. Grace told him about how close she was to her mom, how even though she got a little insistent at times, Mom was practically her best friend, how hard it had been for her sister to marry and have a family and to feel like the black sheep because she wasn't.

Grace told him about the degree in English literature she'd gotten and how useless it was, but that she didn't regret getting it because that degree meant she'd gotten to study important, timeless works of classic literature, which she loved.

"No wonder you can't find a job," he'd joked at that.

She'd smacked his leg playfully before laying her head on his shoulder.

They talked about his childhood racing through the halls of a much smaller version of this inn, of his parents and how they'd supported his crazy ambition to rodeo, of the time he'd gotten bucked from a crazed stallion and had nearly been trampled. They talked about his wife, how much he missed her, how much it had hurt to lose his daughter before she'd even been born.

"I'm so sorry," Grace told him. "I can't even imagine." She hesitated only for a moment. They'd reached such a warm level of emotional intimacy, she hoped he would take what she was going to say in the right light. "Boone, I know I didn't know your wife, but I doubt she would want you to hide away. It's okay to live your life, and there's no better time than Christmas to find healing. If it were me, I would want you to find happiness, even if I wasn't there."

Maybe that was why he was here. Maybe deep down he wanted to awaken from the sleep he'd drifted in for far too long.

He swallowed, but he didn't argue with her. Grace took that as encouraging and went on.

"Maybe that's why the radio played for us."

He leaned his head against hers and groaned. "Not you too."

"Me too?"

"Junie has been going on about it."

Grace lifted a single shoulder. "Junie hasn't said anything, but I did overhear this random couple arguing. They warned me that if I heard music coming from the radio, I needed to run."

Boone chuckled at this, and Grace went on. "They told me the radio thinks it's some kind of matchmaker and that you and I aren't the only ones who've heard it," Grace said, staring at their entwined hands. "The girl said she talked to Junie about it, and Junie said any time anyone heard music come from the radio, strange things happened in people's lives. Some of them ended up married."

"I know. I've heard the stories my whole life. But marriage is a normal thing."

"The events themselves are normal enough, but the circumstances?" She remembered Lacie claiming a snowman had pronounced her and Jared man and wife. That was anything but normal.

"Junie tried to convince me of this too," he said. He lifted his head from hers, and though there wasn't distance between them physically, she felt it increase in other ways. "But even if the radio made the snow fall the way it did so we would be snowed in together, even if a magical song we both happened to hear is exerting the forces of nature to bring us together, that doesn't mean we don't have a choice. But we're in the mountains, Grace," he said with a crooked smile. "It snows here."

She shook her head and adjusted her weight so she no longer sat right next to him but across. "I only took my notebook out once at your cottage, Boone. I'm not sure how it got left there, let alone how it ended up being left behind for you to read. It was in my bag when we left, but when I brought my bag back here, it was gone."

She'd heard the chime in the air, and after talking things over with Junie and Lacie, and now hearing where he'd found the notebook, what else was she supposed to think? For some reason, Santa Claus—wherever he was—believed they should be together. Who was she to argue with Santa and an enchanted radio?

She tilted in to kiss Boone's cheek. But his arms lowered. His brow snapped down, and he reared himself away from her reach. "You should have said something."

She couldn't figure out this sudden change in him. "About... the radio?" They'd talked about it a few times already.

Boone's eyes closed as if he was praying for patience. He exhaled long and hard. "I'm such an idiot. What are we doing here?"

He was angry? "What's wrong with that?" she asked. "I thought you said you were a believer."

He slid off the bed. The floorboards creaked beneath his steps as he paced away from her toward the door. His shoulders hunched, and he paused to rest a hand on the wall and speak over his shoulder to her. "I am. I believe in magic, Grace. That's the problem."

"How can that be a problem?" Things were slipping away from her grasp, too rapidly for her to understand. He'd said he knew they only had tonight? Why was he pulling away again?

"I'm such an idiot," he said again.

Grace rose to her feet and padded toward him. "You are not an idiot. Tonight has been amazing. I don't get what the problem here is."

"I'm an idiot because I forgot."

"You forgot?"

"About magic. About this between us."

"What's wrong with it?"

"We've been pushed together by a magical radio, Grace. I've been able to fight off feelings for every other woman for three years now, except you."

"So?"

"So that makes me think what I'm feeling for you isn't real at all."

His words were a thunderclap. Just minutes before he'd told her how wantable she was—and now he was taking it back? "How can this not be real? I've never felt anything so strong for anyone before."

"Exactly." He sniffed and lifted his hands, only to lower them again. The distance she'd been sensing between them increased, his wall gradually building back up brick by brick.

Grace attempted to figure out his mood swing, but nothing about this abrupt shift in his demeanor made any sense at all. He risked ruining Harper's Inn's landscape by traveling via snowmobile just to rush here, to see her again and return her notebook. He'd admitted how she made him feel. And now he was denying it?

He backed away another step, closer to the door. His retreat wasn't only physically farther from her, but she felt the close connection they'd been building since he made his gallant arrival drifting. "The pass should be cleared tomorrow," he said, a hard shift in his voice. "You should be able to catch your flight."

Tears stung her eyes. "Boone. Don't do this."

"None of this was real. It never was, not from the minute we heard that blasted radio play. I'm sorry. Goodbye, Grace." He turned on his heel. She followed him out to the inn's entrance. The door jingled as he thrust it open and Grace allowed the frigid air to overtake her as she watched him storm down the stairs, kick his snowmobile to life, and drive it back through the trees.

20

The tears came unbidden. Her breathing was choppy and shallow. At least the majority of the guests had gone to the bonfire; Grace would have been mortified if any of them—including Junie or Lacie—witnessed her pathetic dash to the privacy of her room.

The instant she closed the door behind her, she sank onto the bed. Heartache and emotional whiplash were *not* the purposes of this trip. What was she doing? She should be glad Boone broke things off for good between them. That would make things so much easier. She could go home, go on more of her mom's blind dates, and stare at a computer screen all day for the rest of her life in the most boring job anyone could devise.

But the thought of going back to her lonely cubicle grew heavier with every passing hour. She didn't want to go back to that life. Though she'd only been in Montana for a handful of days, that time was enough to let her know she wanted something different. Not just a relationship with a man like Boone. She wanted to live somewhere she could breathe—really breathe. Where she could make her own decisions without her mom second guessing everything. Where she didn't have to deal with the weight of customers shouting at her or go home to an empty, hollow apartment.

Boone and Harper's Inn had presented another side of life she'd never considered before. A side where nature was as necessary as breathing, where it was okay to slow down and enjoy the world around her. If she was going to be staring at a computer screen for her job, she wanted it to be while writing one of the many books crashing around in her brain. She wanted a different life.

"Crying about it won't do any good," she grumbled, fighting the trembling in her lower lip and wiping the tears from her cheeks. "Ugh, now I sound like my mother."

As if sensing as much over wavelengths and the miles between them, her phone chirped from where she'd tossed it onto the bed. Grace sniffed and scanned for the caller. Mom's name appeared. It was stupid to think it might be Boone—he didn't even have her number. Nor had he asked her for it.

"Stupid," she told herself. How could she have let herself get so attached to him when he clearly didn't want any attachment to her? He'd only come to bring her back her notebook.

Sure, and ruined the entire surrounding landscape with snowmobile tracks because he told her he couldn't let her go. She didn't grasp how he could think the time they'd shared together meant nothing.

What was scaring him so badly? So what if it was magic that got them together? Was the idea of being with her so horrid? She refused to believe this overarching, sudden obsession with all things Boone was fake. If that were the case, she wouldn't be a sobbing mess right now.

Grace ignored her phone long enough that the call ended and her mom made a second attempt. Rolling her eyes, sniffing the excess dripping from her nose from crying so hard, Grace swiped the screen and braced herself for the lecture.

She'd forgotten to let her mom know she wouldn't make it home in time. Undoubtedly, that was the purpose of this call.

"Hi, Mom."

"He's here with a date!" Mom fumed without even saying hello.

Grace blinked. Mom's exclamation was enough to shake her to attention. She rolled onto her back and stared upward. "Who is?"

"Terry! He was supposed to be here to meet you but, instead, he brought someone with him. I guess this woman is his girl-friend and he's been dating her for a while. If that was the case, why would Uncle Mike tell me otherwise?"

Grace glanced at the clock and laughed. She laughed and laughed, and the sound was so humorless and cold it struck even her. According to the clock, it was about the time for Mom's Christmas Eve party, and for the expected guests to come. She hadn't given it much thought since being at Boone's, but she let the laughter overtake her. The release was exactly what she needed right now after having her emotions weigh so heavily on her.

The radio was behind this. It had to be. She waited for the chiming sound to alert her of magical interference, but nothing came. She glanced hopefully outside, waiting for the sound of a snowmobile to alert her of Boone's change of mind, but nothing.

Maybe she'd been wrong about everything. What if this wasn't the radio at all, but just further proof of how unwantable she was? She'd said it before—rejection was her lot in life. This was no exception. She'd been rejected by a man she hadn't even wanted to meet in the first place!

"Even though we're all wondering why your plane never

landed, at least you didn't rush home for disappointment," Mom said, sounding disappointed enough for them both.

No, Grace had plenty of that around here. It was almost laughable. She'd told Boone she was unwantable. While the rose of what she wanted was eye-catching and alluring, it was unreachable through all the thorns. Rejection stung everywhere she touched. "It's okay, Mom. Really. I'm sorry I didn't let you know, but a snowstorm hit this area and closed the pass. From what I hear it won't be open until tomorrow."

"Do planes fly on Christmas?" Mom asked.

Grace was touched by this. "You really want me there, don't you?"

"You're my daughter," Mom said, as if this was the most obvious thing, which it was. "It's not the same when you're not here. I thought I'd be okay with you gone for the holiday, but I'm not."

"Mom," Grace said with resignation. Before the sleigh ride, she wasn't sure she'd ever have the guts to say what she needed to say. But Grace was tired of feeling rejected and like she was constantly walking on eggshells. She'd always considered her mom to be one of her best friends, and most of the time she loved being around her. But right now Grace felt so torn and she couldn't hold back her feelings any longer. "You know how restricting my job is, and how badly I want to be a full-time writer."

"I know, honey."

"I'm a grown woman. It's not selfish for me to take my only time off to go after my goals."

"Gracie, you know that's not what I meant."

"Do I, though? Every conversation I've had with you since I got here has been one big guilt trip. I feel like you don't care that I've been having the time of my life here." Up until tonight.

"Stephanie didn't even know I wasn't in Arizona when I called her. She assumed I'd be there because you were already banking on the fact that you could get me to come home. That's not fair. Your happiness shouldn't trump mine, and it wasn't fair for you to guilt trip me into leaving the present that *you* gave me."

Mom paused.

"I came here to work on my book, and it seems like everything has been amazing but upside-down all at once." Grace inhaled long and hard, trying to keep control of her emotions when they wanted to take over.

"I'm sorry," Mom finally said.

Grace sniffed.

Mom's voice changed into a deeper, sincere tone and she exhaled. "Sweetie, you're absolutely right. I'm so sorry, I was being selfish. I didn't mean to put pressure on you to ruin your trip. You're absolutely right. Forget I said anything. Can you still stay, or have you already booked your flight home?"

"It's booked," Grace said, her breath rattling as she tried to get it under control. "I don't think there's any changing it now, not after all the trouble the airline went through to accommodate those of us who got snowed in here. "

Maybe Grace should have just stayed home. None of this emotional rollercoaster with Boone would have happened if she'd stayed home.

"I'm sorry, Gracie Goose. Can you please forgive me?"

The admission touched Grace to the core. "Of course I forgive you. I love you."

"I love you too, honey. I'll try to be more sensitive to your needs, but I am glad you're coming home. I know I've been terribly selfish, but I mean it when I say I've missed you."

The admission struck Grace. This was exactly what she needed to hear. It was like a wake-up call. She had a family who loved her, a family who would never let her down no matter what else was going wrong in her life. Sure, she and Mom had had a misunderstanding, but Grace knew when it came down to it, Mom would always be there for her.

Suddenly, she wanted to leave this bedazzling, beautiful inn.

"Thanks, Mom. I miss you too."

"Oh, sweetie."

"I do. Thanks for loving me and wanting me around." The words made her lip quiver. She fought away the emotion all over again. Stupid feelings of rejection.

Mom didn't respond right away. "Honey, where is this coming from?"

A sniff. "Just my mood." She forced a smile, hoping it transferred to her tone so her mom wouldn't worry. They said goodbye and Grace hung up, thoughts of Boone rampaging through her.

She'd been right. Men in fiction were so much better than men in real life. The real-life ones were confusing and sullen and amazing and kissed like the glow of moonlight on the water. And when she'd had his attention, when he opened up to her and kept her warm, and shared parts of himself and his difficult past with her, it made her soar. Made her feel more special than the sparkle on snow.

Which was probably why his retreat and rejection felt like he'd ripped her heart from her chest. No, she was right. Real life men were both hassle and heartache. Definitely better to stick to book boyfriends. Characters in books always seemed to be more resilient than she was.

There was one thing she needed—or at least, wanted—to do before she left. After hanging up the phone, Grace ventured out to the patio and was pleased to find the hot tub empty. Everyone else was at the bonfire, and that suited her just fine.

She soaked in the toasty warm water, heating her bones

before heading back inside to write out her sorrows. Emotions always fed her writing, and she cashed into the experiences of being at America's North Pole and filled page after page on her laptop, letting herself get lost in the story so she didn't have to think about how badly her own was going.

21

Christmas morning was afresh with glitter and snow light. Grace's resolution allowed her to sleep more soundly than she had in a long time, and the bed's comfort, the utter warmth encasing her, and the pleasant shades of light beaming in from the window, dancing on her eyelids, and the friendly sight of her miniature Christmas tree from its place in the corner of her room all brought a smile to her face.

The smile didn't last long. The minute she awoke, her thoughts instantly clicked in Boone's direction and turned solemn. A lonely, handsome confusing man, waking up in a lonely cabin. Without a Christmas tree. Without any efforts at happiness, a man whose only purpose in life was to shut out anything good that came his way.

Sadness filled her. Sadness for him. He'd been mourning for so long that he didn't know how to let that go. He'd clearly tried. And clearly, that effort had unraveled him. If Grace couldn't help him see that it was okay to let her into his life, then no amount of tinkling music or Santa-led snowstorms could.

Grace was so comfortable in her bed, she didn't want to move. Moving meant letting cold air touch her skin. It meant minutes passing and getting dressed and boarding a plane and leaving this living daydream.

She sat up and checked her phone. Mom texted a picture of herself holding baby Molly. *Merry Christmas, Gracie girl! Can't wait to see you!*

Grace chuckled and remembered why she wanted to leave. Man, she couldn't fault Boone for having his emotions all over the place. Hers were playing ping pong inside of her.

Save some baby snuggles for me! Grace replied.

She wanted to hug her phone. Leaving was better. She'd been entranced here the minute she'd arrived, and she needed to let that go. To let any hope of a life with Boone go.

With an inhale, Grace left the blankets' warmth and trod to the shower. She basked in the warm water, then dressed in a festive red shirt—telling herself she needed to invest in more sweaters were she ever to come back here. Christmas morning was the perfect day for a cozy sweater.

She blew her hair dry and took her time shaping it with loose curls. She powdered her face and applied mascara and lip gloss. When she stepped from the room, the hall was bright with activity. Guests came and went, smiling as they did so. A pair of children drove a remote-control car down the hall, and the sound of their laughter burst with its own kind of magic.

Down the stairs—after a quick peek and a greeting in at the now-silent radio—Grace tread into the dining room. Festive music played overhead from a more updated sound system and from a newer era than what had come from the radio. Families gathered at the tables, opening gifts, sharing hugs, laughing and enjoying their meals.

Grace's heart gave a twinge. She could see why Boone avoided this place during Christmas. Family happened here, loud and clear. Family and happiness and cheer. All the things he'd lost.

If only he allowed himself to believe he hadn't lost them forever.

Situated at a table near the door, Junie sat beside a man with black hair and a white overcoat that had a little bit of food spilled on it. Hmm, looked like the chef was taking a break. Junie touched his arm. He said something to which she threw her head back and laughed, and then he stood and headed for the kitchen once more.

Lacie and Jared were nowhere in sight, but Grace still wondered how their Christmas was going after having their circumstances change so rapidly and in such an...interesting way. Married by a snowman? That was a story not many people would believe.

Grace sipped her hot chocolate, loving the surge of warmth plunging straight to her belly with satisfying effect. She relished this, wanting to take in as much as she could. Because to every happy inhale she drew in, an opposite exhale left her body. This was her last morning here. She'd called the airline. Once the pass opened, she was boarding a plane.

Every time a person stood from his or her table, every time someone entered the dining room, every time they left, she foolishly hoped it was Boone. Maybe he would change his mind and come charging back across the countryside on his snowmobile. Maybe he would whisk her away to his cottage for a final hour together. Maybe he...

But no. He wasn't coming. He hadn't changed after all. He was still clinging to the notion that he was better off hiding his heart. That was why he refused to accept that his feelings were real. And if she wanted to protect hers from him, she had to do the same.

Junie stood from her table and called to the room. "Excuse me, everyone? Can I have your attention please?"

The chatter quieted. The children stilled, being urged back

to their families' tables. Some went willingly. Others took more coercion, but either way, Junie beamed at the room at large.

"Good morning, and Merry Christmas!" she called.

A few people clapped and many people, including Grace, called, "Merry Christmas!" in return.

"After last night's festivities, I hope you've all stayed nice and warm and gotten a good night's sleep."

Several people laughed. Grace wondered what she'd missed at the bonfire.

Junie went on, holding her phone into the air. "I have some good news. For those of you wanting to venture into West Hills this morning, our sleighs and cars can now make it through. They've cleared the pass!"

Cheers greeted this, along with more applause. The announcement turned the cocoa in Grace's stomach sour. She wanted this, right? She wanted to leave.

Junie continued her announcement, explaining how someone named Troy would be available with the sleigh after breakfast for those who wanted to venture into town on a Christmas ride. And while families celebrated and enjoyed their breakfasts together, Grace slipped back to her room.

It didn't take long to pack her things. Soon, she had her suitcase handle in hand, her bag over her shoulder, but she couldn't manage to reach for the knob. She waited, praying for the sound of mystical, festive chimes to hover in the air around her, to make necklaces appear or to bring Boone to her door.

But there was no music. And there was no Boone.

Grace gave her room a final glance. Nostalgia filled her chest. "I'm sorry," she told the room. "But I lied when I said I wanted to go home."

She would miss this charming, wonderful place. But at least she'd captured it in her story. She'd gotten a good ten thousand words written during her emotional ranting last night, and that was serious progress.

A thought struck. On a whim, Grace pulled her bag from her shoulder and retrieved her notebook. She didn't stop to think. Pen in hand, she wrote what was in her heart.

Boone,

I'm leaving this morning, but I want you to know I'll never forget you or what happened between us. I don't know about you, but the music from that radio changed my life for the better. It led me to a man better than I knew he could be. A man I never thought would pay any attention to me. A man with a good heart and who will be in my dreams for years to come.

I'm writing this because I want you to know why I love Christmas. I love it because it brings families together. Much as I loathe to leave Harper's Inn, I'm going home to spend the holiday with my family, which I should have done in the first place.

You haven't lost every good thing in your life, Boone. You only lose good things if you push them away when they come to you. And I'm still here.

I'll never forget you. If you feel like you could give me a chance, I would like to see you again. Merry Christmas. And I mean that.

Grace

She added her email and phone number to the bottom of the note, folded it with a prayer, and wrote his name across the front.

Grace gave the room a final glance and then, with a resolved sigh, she wheeled her suitcase out into the hall. Down the stairs. And she stopped at the reception desk, where Junie awaited with a pair of reindeer ears on her head. She gave Grace a wide grin.

"Hey, Grace. Merry Christmas."

"Merry Christmas to you, Junie." Grace placed her key on the counter. Junie took it and added them back onto the hook on the wall to her right. She swiped on her tablet screen and tapped a few things before returning her glance to Grace.

"You're all set," Junie said. "All checked out."

Grace pressed her lips into a smile. "Thanks for everything. I'll never forget this place." Or the attractive, closed-off sleigh driver. Grace turned to leave, but a wedge in her chest kept her feet in place. It was now or never. She faced Junie once more.

"You haven't heard anything from him?" Grace asked.

From the insightful twinkle and compassion in Junie's expression, she grasped more than she let on. How much did Junie know about that old radio? "Nothing. I'm sorry, Grace."

Grace inhaled a long, deep, draw of cinnamon-infused air into her lungs. She rifled into her coat pocket and retrieved the note she'd written. "Can you at least leave this for him?"

Junie placed her hand on the note and slid it toward herself. "Now that I can do."

The two women exchanged nods. And then, with her heart in her throat and a final gaze at Harper's Inn, Grace zipped up her coat and stepped outside. Her Uber driver helped place her suitcase in the trunk, and then he descended down the mountain and she made her way to the airport to fly home.

22

Boone was a fool. He'd run away from his and Amy's home in Deer Lodge because he couldn't bear the reminders of her in every tree, every stoplight, and every corner of their apartment. And now he'd gone and gotten closer to Grace Eastland than he ever intended to, and she was everywhere he looked too. She was in the trees, in the mountainside and the sky, in the snowmobile tracks on the snow Junie still continued to curse him for.

"Tell me again what you're doing in here?" Junie demanded.

This room was the worst place of all—apart from his cottage where he still envisioned that night by the fire and the morning she'd woken with dreams in her lashes and invitation in her glances. He couldn't bear to be home, not when she was everywhere. So he'd come to the inn earlier than ever before the day after Christmas and had exerted himself in every task that had needed looking into for a while now. The creak in the stairs leading up to the attic. The leak in the kitchen ceiling.

He couldn't up and leave the inn for good, not when his family had entrusted the cottage to him and when Junie relied so much on him to help her around here. So his next best option was staying busy. Several days had passed since he started these repairs, and he found he still needed something to keep him occupied.

"We're taking down that tree." He gestured to the eyesore with too much tulle in the corner of the inn's living room.

She folded her arms. "No, we're leaving it there until after New Years'."

"No. It's coming down. Christmas is over."

"Only for you," Junie argued. "Believe it or not, other people like to continue celebrating for a few more days. They *like* Christmas, Boonie."

"Don't call me that."

"What? That's you and me. Boonie and Junie."

"Yeah, when we were ten."

She glared at him. "Lighten up."

His frown deepened. He turned his attention to the other part of this room that caused him irritation. The radio stood on the table in all its accursed glory, looking innocent, though it was anything but. "And don't even get me started on this thing. I take it things are going well with you and Mason?"

"Where did that come from?" Junie asked.

"Why else would you have brought that radio back down here after I tried hiding it away?" His tone was too gruff, and he knew it, but he couldn't help being irritated with her. What was wrong with women who were so enraptured by romance that they'd hand their lives over to some unknown source? None of them had a clue why the radio started to play this year. None of them knew who was behind it—not really. Putting their trust in something like that was the worst kind of idiocy he could think of.

He was only glad he'd let Grace go.

Junie stilled. He felt her gaze penetrate his profile before slowly allowing his to meet it, and when he did, he rolled his eyes.

"Don't look at me like that, Juniper Harper."

"Don't call me Juniper Harper."

"Why not? You're resorting to ridiculous childish names. And that is your name."

He turned to the tree, trying to decide where to start. If he had it his way, all of this would go in the garbage. They could forego the holiday altogether. Guests would find other reasons to come here and stay—but he knew Christmas was a big draw to this inn in particular because of the story his family had spouted all over since starting the place.

Junie spoke to his back. "I didn't bring the radio back down here. I came down the next morning and it was there. I assumed you moved it."

"Ludicrous."

"It hasn't played in a hundred years, Boone."

"You think I don't know that?"

"It had to have started this year for a reason."

"It's fake!" he shouted, letting his frustration boil over. A few guests passed by the front room, and when he shot his scowl in their direction, they ducked their heads and hurried on.

"Great, scare away all the guests, why don't you?" Junie frowned. "First snowmobile tracks and now this." Her lips held a smirk. She was trying to get him to ease up, but he didn't want to. He'd had so much rage boiling inside of him, for so long. So much repressed emotion he'd pushed down and kept out of sight. It wasn't fair to let it all out at her—he knew that. But that outburst had come from nowhere.

"Sorry," he muttered.

"What's the matter? Is it because of Grace?"

He rolled his eyes. "You had to bring her up."

"Do you miss her?"

"I'm not talking about her right now." He pulled at some of the ridiculous tulle on the tree. A few bulbs clattered to the ground, but thankfully, they were new ones Junie had bought rather than the original glass ones belonging to their grandparents that were stored in the attic.

He waited for Junie's reproach, but she strolled from the room and returned minutes later with one of her large totes. It was labeled *Christmas Tree*, and he chuckled at that. The year she'd gotten those, he'd tried helping her label them. He'd labeled it *X-Mas Tree,* and she'd scolded him.

"Keep Christ in Christmas," she'd said, putting a new label on the tote.

He'd never forgotten that. He couldn't forget. But he could praise his Savior without all of this other nonsense. Nonsense that Junie and so many others insisted on. That was why the fact that she wasn't stopping him...stopped him.

She'd made it clear she wasn't happy he was in here tearing things down so early. And yet, she was helping him, of all things. Junie manned the other side of the tree and helped him untwine the tulle until it collected into a large sparkly green wad in her arms. "I think it's not all fake," she said from behind the wad.

Boone removed a few of the bulbs and placed them in the tote. "What?"

"The radio. The music. The magic. It's not fake, Boone."

Her comment sparked something inside of him. What did she mean by that? What had happened with her and Mason since they'd heard the radio play for them?

"Do you hear chiming every time the two of you get forced to be together?" His voice was low and sarcastic. A few other guests passed by and peered into the living room, but they didn't stop or complain that the tree was being taken down. Thank goodness. With the mood he was in, he probably would have lost it on them too.

Junie's mouth screwed in that little way she had whenever she was thinking. She tilted her head so one of the bells sticking up from the headband she wore jingled. "I wouldn't say it's all forced. Maybe at first it was. I mean, I told you we would end up standing here in front of the radio and not remembering the actual walking there. But we're on day nine now. Now we seek each other out and wait for the radio to play."

A tickle of emotion pestered the center of his chest. His interest piqued. Mason was on board with this now? Had she explained everything to him? Maybe he didn't realize the radio was still manipulating them. "So it's not messing with your lives?"

Junie's lips spread into a goofy, love-struck smile. Her eyes drifted out the window, and she lost herself in some kind of memory. Color flushed her cheeks, and she chewed her bottom lip. "Oh, it is," she said, squeaking out another grin.

"How so?"

Junie rolled her eyes and stepped close enough to shove the tulle into his arms. The jingle bells on her head tinkled again. He did his best to keep the gnarled heap from slipping and then transferred it to the tote. That was a mess. No doubt, Junie would organize it later.

Instead of griping at him over her usually perfectly organized decorations, she dug into the back pocket of her jeans and retrieved something small, folded, and white. "You're getting into some personal questions, Boonie. Here." She gripped his wrist, yanked it forward, and slapped the paper into Boone's palm. "Read this and tell me if you think this was all just some short-lived, magic trance for you and Grace."

Boone's fist tightened over the note. What was Junie talking about now? His heart began to race against his will. "You— what? She left this?"

Hands on her hips, Junie gestured with an elbow. "For you. See for yourself."

He opened his fist and flattened out the paper. Sure enough, his name was scrawled on the note. He recognized her pretty handwriting from reading a little bit of it in her notebook. She was careful in her scrawl, careful and precise. Something attempted to push its way through the solid walls of his heart, but he gritted his teeth and forced it away.

"Not happening," he said, bitterly tucking the note into his pocket.

Junie's mouth dropped. "Seriously? You won't even read it?"

"Did you read it?"

"What do you think?" She rolled her eyes and glanced around the mess Boone had made in the usually pristine room. "You know what? I'll leave you to this. I don't need the purge." She kicked the tote and stormed from the room.

Boone couldn't grasp what made Junie so upset or why she thought anything that had happened since the day before Christmas Eve was real. There was a reason no one believed in Santa Claus anymore. All the folklore, all the hype, the talk and claims of magic, could all be explained away. One man visiting all the homes in the world in a single night. Reindeer flying. It was all nonsense.

Boone had always claimed to be a believer, but what did he believe in, really? He believed the story he'd been told as a child. His grandfather was sitting in front of the fireplace, watching the flames dance. Grandpa Harper held the orange he'd received for Christmas in his hand and attempted not to feel sorry for himself because he hadn't gotten the toy train he'd asked for.

Then the fire had gusted out. A knock had sounded on the door. Not from the chimney. The door.

In confusion, Grandpa Harper rose and answered to find a man in a white beard and a hat not unlike the one Grace had worn—not red, but long and pointed with a pom-pom at the end, dangling down his shoulder. The radio was in his arms.

"Merry Christmas, my young friend," St. Nick had said. "Mind if I come in from the cold?"

Grandpa Harper had let the stranger in and the two had gone to stand in front of the fire.

"Sorry, sir," Grandpa Harper had been rumored to say. "The fire's just gone out."

"I'll take care of that," St. Nick said. With a finger to the side of his nose, the fire burst into life, flickering more orange and wilder than before. Grandpa Harper claimed he saw flames laced with sparkles.

"Whoa!" Grandpa Harper said, standing in amazement. He'd never been so entranced or so warm. The fire gave off more than heat—it filled the room with magic. Grandpa Harper had sworn, even in his old age, he could still remember the smell and the tingle of it on his skin.

"There now," St. Nick had said, bending before the young boy. "How is that for warmth?"

"Wonderful," Grandpa Harper said. "Who are you?"

"I am St. Nicholas."

"I'm—"

"No need to tell me yours," St. Nick claimed. "I know you're Benjamin Harper."

Grandpa Harper nodded enthusiastically, wondering who this stranger really was and how he knew his name. Back then, it wasn't quite so weird for random people to be welcomed into a person's home, especially if that person needed help. Which, this far north in Montana, strangers often did. Harper's Inn was the only place around for miles.

"Now then, Benjamin," St. Nicholas said. "I'm only passing through, but I believe I've made a terrible mistake."

"I hate when I mess up," Grandpa Harper had said.

The older man's nose was quite rosy by this point in time. He smiled, though his lips weren't very visible through his bushy white mustache and beard. "So do I. I've come to make things right. Tell me, Benjamin. Did you get many presents for Christmas?"

When Grandpa Harper had told the story, he would emphatically frown and exaggerate his facial expressions. "No, but I'm all right."

"It's good to keep our promises," St. Nicholas said. "I've made a stop at every house in the world this year, except yours. And I'm afraid my elves have completely run out of gifts. Even the train you asked for. But I promised to deliver, and deliver I shall."

That was how Boone knew as a child that this story was legit. There was no way the stranger could know both Grandpa Harper's name *and* what he'd asked Santa for on his Christmas list.

St. Nicholas knelt in front of Grandpa Harper. Boone remembered the way he would always slide forward, anticipating this most exciting part of Grandpa's story.

"I'm afraid I have nothing else to give you but this old radio. It isn't much, but it can still bring you joy. Do you like music, Benjamin?"

"I do!" Grandpa Harper exclaimed. Boone could still recollect the twinkle in his grandfather's eyes as he used to relay this.

St. Nicholas patted his cheek. He stepped aside and then placed the same hand on the radio. "This came from my own house. It wasn't something built in my workshop. This is something I crafted myself, lad. It can play the jolliest tunes. But it can also play tricks."

"Like magic tricks?" Grandpa Harper had asked.

"Something like that," St. Nicholas said. After Grandpa Harper thanked him for the gift, St. Nicholas left the way he'd come. Through the front door. Junie had it right; the radio was rumored to have played that first year, and while Grandma Harper and Junie talked about the weddings that followed, Boone couldn't remember specifically the things people claimed had happened.

If only Grandpa Harper were still around to talk to. The more time passed, Boone wasn't sure he knew what he believed anymore. That could have been a story Grandpa made up. He'd always been a good storyteller.

Boone shook his head. He knew that wasn't the case. Nothing else could explain why the radio had played for him and Grace that night. He clenched the note in his fist again, tempted to chuck it into the fire.

For all he knew, the note had just appeared to Junie like the notebook did to him. Appeared, like magic. Which meant that whatever was on it didn't mean anything. Grace would never have written any of it if the radio hadn't interfered.

No matter what either of them said, this wasn't real.

Boone stuffed the note in his pocket, determined to forget it was there. Once the holidays passed, he would prove it. He would stop thinking about Grace every second, stop reliving the feel of her lips or the sound of her honeyed voice or the way she made him want conversation and company again, the way she had tried to help him heal.

23

G race pressed a finger against her headset as though she needed the stability of keeping it in place. She stared at the numbers on her screen so long they blended together. Soon, her mind drifted. She was back in Montana, daydreaming of a cowboy recluse and a snowy mountainside.

"Excuse me? Are you still there?" The other woman on the line sounded more concerned than anything else.

Grace shook herself from the clouds and took in the cubicle and the screen that didn't have her novel on it and jerked. "Oh, yes. I'm sorry, I'm here. What did you say?"

The woman on the line repeated her complaint, mentioning how the company's newest line of skin care made her eyes itch. She wanted a refund. Of course. They all did.

"I'm sorry to hear that, ma'am," Grace said, kicking her brain back into gear and beginning the refund process. She talked the woman through returning the product and emailed the print-ready prepaid shipping label. Much as she wanted to lose herself in thoughts of Boone and the memorable holiday she'd shared with him, much as she wished she could quit and just write the story currently bouncing in her brain and begging to be written, she still had bills to pay.

Ordinary life was so dull without Christmas carols and the lights she'd strung along her cubicle. She wished every day could be like Christmas. Wasn't it ironic that the man she'd fallen for happened to hate the holiday so much he devoted his life to hiding from it and from anyone who reminded him that it was meant to be a happy time of year?

"Forget him," Grace told herself as she hung up with the customer and filled out the necessary notes from each and every single call she received. "Focus on your book."

That had been hard enough to do since she'd returned home. She'd spent every second she could with Stephanie and her adorable, squishy, giggly baby. They'd talked long into the night on Christmas. Stephanie's husband had stopped asking when Stephanie was going to come to bed after a while. Grace had even gotten up to help with the baby because they were still up talking. And though she'd confessed her short-lived romance with Boone, Grace omitted anything about hearing the radio play. Stephanie's reactions were enough without adding that part to it.

Every time she opened her laptop to clack in a few more words, the email icon screamed at her to contact him. Even if she had the guts to reach out, Boone had given her no way to contact him. Emailing the inn felt so silly because Junie would be the one who received it. Not him.

Grace had already left a note for him with Junie anyway. No need to make herself appear more desperate than she already did. They were nearing the end of January. If Junie had given the note to him, he would have tried to contact Grace by now, wouldn't he? Or maybe Junie decided not to give Boone her note, though why she wouldn't was beyond Grace. She supposed she would never know.

Boone hadn't contacted her.

He probably never would.

She really needed to move on.

Grace had been hesitant to answer in the affirmative to Mom's invitation about another blind date tonight. On impulse, Grace reached for her phone and gave the delayed reply: *Okay, I'll do it.*

You don't sound all that excited, Mom answered.

How do you know what I sound like? It's a text.

That was the wrong thing to say. The minute Grace clocked out after work ended, while walking to her rusted red Ford in January's almost seventy-degree evening, her phone rang.

Grace swiped to answer. "Hey, Mom."

"Hi sweetie. So good to hear your voice. Texting really has its merits, but you're right. Conversations in person are much better."

She wasn't sure when she'd ever said anything like that, but clearly, Mom had construed as much from their conversation. "What's up, Mom?"

"I have a better idea than a blind date," Mom said.

Grace fumbled with her bag but managed to retrieve her keys and unlock the door. She chucked her bag into the empty passenger seat and slid inside. "What's that?"

"How about a mother-daughter date?" Mom said. "Just you and me. Like old times."

Growing up, Mom had taken her out quite a bit, for back-to-school shopping or to get dinners on nights when Dad was gone for work and Mom didn't want to cook. Grace's heart swelled at the suggestion. She missed those days.

"You know, that would be great."

"Perfect," Mom said. "Have you had dinner yet?"

"Not yet. Just got off work."

"What sounds good to you?" They chatted for a few minutes

about a location and then agreed to meet there. Grace didn't mind not returning to her empty apartment first. She was grateful for the change in monotony.

She drove through town and pulled into the parking lot of their favorite sandwich place. Grace lingered in her car, checking her email on her phone, and then emerged once she caught sight of Mom's golden minivan. She'd given Mom a hard time for picking such a big vehicle when it was only ever Grace since her sister married and moved away. But Mom always insisted she needed the space.

"Hey, my Gracie girl," Mom said, pulling Grace into a hug. She hadn't been one on one with Mom since Christmas. Knowing Grace was fully ensconced in finishing her novel, they'd passed or popped in but nothing more extensive than that.

"Hey, where's Dad?"

"Working late," Mom said. She made it to the door first and opened it. Grace smiled and entered, taking in the delectable taste of freshly baked bread smattered with spices. They ordered and then took their usual spot by the back window where they used to people-watch. Grace had always loved doing that. She would come with a notebook and just write down people. What they wore. How they smiled. How they interacted. She would imagine stories between them based on what they carried in their hands or whether they looked at others around them.

She supposed she'd always been one for details.

Mom chewed, and from the lack of conversation, Grace could tell something was up. Grace ate, attempting to savor the spicy mustard on her turkey BLT, but it was no use. No matter how often she glanced away—up to the dangling lights overhead, to the used road signs screwed to the wall adding an eclectic feel to the place, to the massive TVs blasting some sports game or another—every time she peered back, her mom was watching her.

Grace lowered her sandwich. "Okay, for real. What's up?"

Mom lowered her sandwich and wiped her mouth. "It's nothing really. We just haven't really talked since you got back after Christmas."

"We talked at the party," Grace argued.

"Yes, sweetie, but not really *talking*. I mean about important stuff."

Grace's guard raised. "There's nothing to talk about."

"Gracie."

"What?"

"You're different," Mom said. "What happened? Did you meet someone?"

Eye roll. "Is everything about men with you?"

"Of course not. I'm just trying to figure out what's bothering you since you won't tell me."

Grace softened at this. She'd always been pretty open with her mom. It was natural for Mom to suspect something was up if Grace was keeping things to herself. Which she totally was. Grace had told everything but the radio part of things to Stephanie. She hadn't felt the need to fill Mom in. How could she begin to tell about the magic surrounding Harper's Inn? About the radio's bizarre origin story or the way it played without a power source or the way things happened ever since to thrust her and Boone together?

Just like that. She said it just like that.

"I know it sounds crazy," Grace finished. "But I swear, music was in the air during our sleigh ride, Mom. And then the snow picked up out of nowhere. And then one thing led to another and we kissed and just ended up opening our hearts to each other."

"That sounds incredibly romantic, honey. Like, movie-worthy. But he doesn't want a relationship?" Mom asked.

"No." The admission placed a prickly barb right in the center of her throat.

"Because of something in his past?"

Grace sniffed. "That was his excuse at first, but then he came back to the inn. He told me he thought the radio was proving he could love again. And then I told him the things I wrote in the notebook were true and that I believed the radio was helping us be together, and he just backed away. Like it was nothing."

Mom frowned as she chewed, staring at the cup of Dr. Pepper in front of her. Grace could practically see the cogs spinning in her mind. "Sounds like he got scared," Mom said.

"Of what?"

"Commitment?"

Grace pressed her fingers to her temples. "I just don't get how he can be willing to give things a try with me one minute and then push me away the instant I'm ready to do the same. The man has more emotional switchbacks than a mountain road."

"I'm sorry, sweetie." Mom didn't offer any helpful advice. But sometimes a listening ear was worth more than the greatest advice a person could give. That was all Grace needed. She'd been carrying the weight of Boone's whiplash emotions with her since Christmas, and it felt so good to get everything off her chest again—*everything* this time. Radio and all.

More than anything, Mom wasn't calling her off or telling her to stop being ridiculous for believing a magical radio had taken issues into its own hands by pushing couples together.

Conversation shifted again and became easier between them. Mom talked about work, about missing Dad because he was gone so much. Grace reached out a hand.

"I'm sorry I've been so selfish," Grace said. Mom had stayed away purposely to give Grace space enough to write. And even though she hadn't said as much, that had been hard for her.

"You're not selfish. I know your writing is important to you."

"Thanks, Mom, it is. But it's not more important than the people. I forget that sometimes when I'm lost in one of my worlds. Sometimes I emerge from a writing session and have to get a brand-new grasp on reality and remember other people exist." She chuckled.

"Well, you come on over after work any time you want."

"You know, I never really told you how grateful I am for you and Dad."

Mom waved a hand. Grace hurried on. "It's true. When I was so crushed over Boone on Christmas Day, you have no idea how much it meant for me to know I had you. That I still had someone who loved me and would accept me no matter what."

Mom's eyes twinkled. "Of course we love you, Gracie Goose."

Grace fought down the emotion threatening to climb her throat. She zoned in on her sandwich's empty foil in its plastic basket. "That just meant a lot to me, to know you were there when I needed you."

Mom thought this over. "And what about this man of yours? Boone. Where is his family?"

"He works at the inn with his aunt and cousin. He mentioned having a brother, but that's all I know. I think his parents have both passed. His wife and baby died. He's completely alone." Saying the words struck a lonesome chord inside of her.

Mom's face mashed into a sincere, compassionate pout. "Oh, honey. The poor man."

Grace read the sincerity in Mom's eyes and nodded before speaking. "Yeah. He's pretty reclusive as a result of it, I think."

"I'm sure after being alone for so long it can be hard to let people back in. Change is always hard," Mom said.

"Yeah." This conversation turned things in Grace's mind all over again. She hadn't considered that aspect of it. Boone had Junie—but a cousin wasn't quite the same as a mother and father. Or a spouse. "It must have really rattled him to let me get even moderately close to him."

"That doesn't mean it was a mistake," Mom said, firmly and with gusto. She even pressed her finger to the table as if to emphasize her point. "Maybe he just needs more time to adjust to having someone close to him again."

Grace sniffed. She appreciated Mom's unapologetic insight, but she wasn't sure she could completely agree. There had to be a reason Boone continued to pull back from her.

"Maybe we proved the point," Grace said. "Maybe he's better off being on his own, without anyone to love in his life." She didn't want to accept it, but it was the only solution that hurt the least.

"Would you want that for yourself?" Mom's gaze was too direct.

Grace squirmed slightly under its focus. "You know I wouldn't."

Much as she loved her introverted life as a writer, she still missed the bustle of the inn, the feel of coming to life she'd experienced the instant she'd stepped inside. And if she was still there, she wouldn't want to hide away. She would want to be with those she loved the most.

Grace suddenly lost her appetite. She placed what was left of her sandwich back onto its foil.

Mom's hand reached over and grasped Grace's across the table. "You don't have to stay here, Grace. Go back to West Hills. Find a job there, write your books. If Santa's radio pushed you to him, there has to be a reason."

Grace stared at their joined hands for several long seconds

before her lids lifted and she met her mom's kind gaze. "You mean, you believe me?"

Mom pulled her hand away and sat up with a knowing smile. "How else do you explain what you two both heard? Sounds to me like you were given a nudge. Now the rest is up to you."

"Mom—You could barely have me gone over Christmas. How can you stand to have me so far away?"

"Honey, I was only saying that because it was Christmas. I'll be okay. I've got your dad. Besides, this isn't about me. I know you loved it there. That's the one thing I've been able to get you to tell me." She laughed at this. "I also know you hate your job."

"Yeah, but it's a job. I need it."

Mom waved this off. "There are plenty of jobs to be found. Go. Find your life. Make sure it's the life you dream of because something tells me that life isn't here."

Grace's heart threatened to burst from her chest. She finished her sandwich with more fervor this time, and just before heading home, she pulled Mom into the biggest hug they'd shared in a while.

"Thank you for this," Grace said. "For everything."

Mom beamed at her. A gleam in her gaze held the same, adoring glint it had always had. A glint of pride. Of gratitude that Grace was her daughter. Grace hadn't realized how much that glint meant to her. "Of course," Mom said. "Just make sure you keep me in the loop."

Grace couldn't believe she was doing this. But everything her mom said during dinner felt so right. She'd never believed in magic before, but that entire situation in Montana had made a believer out of her.

But could she do it? Quit her job, pack up and move to the place where Boone was? Would he leave if she did? Would he give her another chance? The possibility of him rejecting her again was far too fresh. It sank like a boulder into her stomach.

Grace thought it over while driving home. She let the scene play out in her mind as she folded her clothes and changed the sheets on her bed for those that had been freshly laundered. She thought about it when she should have been watching her favorite series on Netflix and ended up missing the impactful details between Jeremy and Sarah and shut off the show in frustration so she didn't miss anything else.

TV off, she gently tossed the remote onto the empty couch cushion beside her. "Empty cushions," she said, staring around. Only her keys hung on the peg by the door. Only her purse dangled on the three available hooks across from the keys. Her shoes sat solitary on the mat. She'd had dinner with her mom tonight, but if Mom hadn't called, chances were that she would have eaten here. By herself.

She pictured Boone doing the same, day after day. Working with Hazelnut, undoing her harness, parking the sleigh and feeding the horse before heading in to his remote, lonely little cottage. Cooking some kind of meal by himself. Eating that meal alone at his table. Sitting by the fire with a book. Empty couch cushions.

Flames filled her chest at the memory of sharing that couch with him. She'd gone from being completely alone and near to freezing in the bedroom, by herself, to joining him, sharing the fire, the light, the blanket. And then, her innermost thoughts —and his.

"He said he believed," she muttered to the room. She needed to help him believe in more than just magic, though.

With that thought, every other thought dropped in her mind like newly fallen snow. A feeling of certainty shook away the fear lodged into her chest. If she chose to stay here in Scottsdale, nothing would ever change. She would come home to an empty apartment, eat all her meals alone, sleep alone, be alone, and then have constant reminders of her aloneness because Mom wouldn't stop trying to set her up.

Boone would be alone too. Drive horses, bicker with Junie, ignore the guests as much as possible, and go to his empty little cottage, living a hollow life.

Or she could act. Make a believer out of him too. A believer in love and second chances at it.

Suddenly, without chiming music or anything out of the ordinary other than a dawning thought, Grace remembered her first night at Harper's Inn. Junie had been the one to come and check her towels and ensure the room was to her liking.

"We're short-staffed," she'd said. Did that mean they were hiring? There was only one way to find out.

The next day, Grace waltzed in to work, headed for her boss's office, and gave her notice. Two weeks would give her time to settle everything, to pack, find someone to buy the contract on her apartment, and contact Junie. She also had just enough time to finish her book. With nervous anticipation, Grace sent the draft off to her beta readers for their feedback.

Before she knew it, she was saying goodbye to her parents and boarding one more plane, carrying a lot more luggage this time. Over the fields she'd go. Not quite laughing all the way, but she couldn't manage to wipe the smile from her face the entire way through security and while waiting at her boarding gate.

The cramped airline seats surrounding her weren't necessarily one-horse open sleighs, but they still made her spirits bright. The idea of a radio from Santa coming to life and spreading Christmas magic through song to bring people love was crazy. So, so crazy.

Even so, no sense in letting a good amount of crazy go to waste.

24

Boone stood in the inn's large dining room with a plastic goblet in hand, holding the sparkling cider being served. He had to admit, he wouldn't have minded something a little stronger, but this was a family inn, a family night to celebrate the new year.

Each of the three large-screened TVs blasted the ball drop in New York City. They had only minutes to go now. Boone couldn't understand the appeal of gathering in Times Square, but then again, it had taken all of Junie's powers of coercion to get him in the dining room tonight instead of burrowing at home.

Children who were up way past their bedtimes were either nestled on their mom's or dad's laps or running amok all over the dining room, weaving in and out of the tables and chairs. Guests sat and chatted in friendly conversation, though Boone didn't fail to notice a few check their phones and yawn.

Lacie and Jared had gone home a few days ago, as had most of the other guests who'd been staying for the Christmas holiday. Boone was glad. He found he could enter the living room much easier without a Christmas tree hoarding the space. Now, it was just a normal room again, and he hardly even glanced in the radio's direction when he entered to check the fires. Just like he used to.

Junie sequestered herself with her mom, Aunt Meg. Boone didn't fail to notice that Mason Devries, the chef, happened to be situated on the other side of the room. Boone frowned, wondering what had happened between them. Last he'd checked, Junie had grinned like an idiot at the mere mention of Mason.

Then again, he knew exactly what had happened. Christmas was over. The radio had stopped playing. Which meant their infatuation was over, just like Boone suspected it would be.

Good thing Grace had left. He'd hate for things to have gotten any more awkward between them than they already had.

As if sensing him watching her, Junie peered behind her. Boone ducked his glance to his shoes, but too late. Junie said something to her mom and then made her way over to him.

"Happy New Year," she said.

"Not quite. A few more minutes."

She sat on the empty chair nearest him. "You know what New Year's means?"

He slid a wry glance to her. "If you're here to talk to me about resolutions, you can skip the lecture."

"Christmas is over," Junie said with a smile, undeterred.

His brows knitted. "I thought we covered that."

"You're still sulking, though."

Boone gritted his teeth. "I am not."

Junie bumped his arm. "Come on, you haven't smiled once tonight. Not even at the little kids. I know you love being around the kids. I've watched you through all the sleigh rides you gave today, and you aren't even teasing anyone."

Boone shrugged this fact off. "I haven't been myself lately," he admitted.

"Because you miss Grace."

He closed his eyes. Was that really all Junie wanted to talk about with him anymore? He wasn't doing this. He wasn't going to talk about Grace. Junie would ask if he'd read that note yet, and he didn't want to admit that he'd tucked it away in his drawer alongside Amy's necklace, unopened.

He also was in no mood for Junie to mention whatever was going on with her and Mason. Boone had had enough of that radio and of talk of Christmas to last him for a lifetime.

Not waiting for midnight, he tipped the sparkling cider back and downed it in one gulp. "Happy New Year, Junie. Good night."

$\sim$

Days passed. Guests came and went, though not as many as they had during the holidays. That didn't bother him, though. This was how things had always gone. The inn's traffic would stay slow again until Valentine's Day, when couples liked to come for a mountain getaway. Then they'd trickle down again until summer when the lake thawed. Then the hayrides and camping parties would pick up. Inevitably, there were family members who had no interest in camping and would bunk at Harper's instead. And undoubtedly, the rooms were already booked for next December by now.

Boone did his best to avoid his cousin at all costs. He spent the majority of his time either in the barn, looking after the horses and repairing dents in the sleighs, or at his cottage, drowning in as many books as he could read.

He couldn't help overhearing conversations though. Junie and Aunt Meg were talking inside Junie's office once while Boone passed with one of her totes of decorations she'd asked him to retrieve.

"I'll be holding interviews this weekend," Junie said as Boone pushed into the office.

He didn't ask about the interviews or what she was referencing. She and Aunt Meg had always handled the inn. He wasn't going to intervene.

On his way out of the office again, Aunt Meg stopped him. "Boone, hang on a second."

He faced her. "What's up?" His aunt looked a lot like her daughter. Tall and thin with freckles and a bit more wrinkles than Junie had.

"You still have all of Grandpa's books at your place, don't you?"

"Yeah. I've been making my way through them." Grandpa Harper had an old collection of stories written in the early 1900s. The writing took some getting used to, but Boone found he enjoyed the stories and their messages.

"Perfect," she said, reaching for an older volume on her desk. "Can you take this and put it with yours? I think it goes along with one of Grandpa's collections."

Excitement slicked through him. He'd made his way through those old books a few times now. "Thanks, Aunt Meg. Having something new to read will be great."

"How are you doing out there, anyway?" Aunt Meg asked. Junie appeared behind her mom's shoulder and watched him with curiosity.

Boone refused to glance at Junie. "Fine. Thanks, I'd better get going."

Aunt Meg smiled and turned back to her desk, and Boone made for the exit.

Junie caught him on the way out. "Hey. If you're looking for something new to read, I have something in mind," she taunted to his back.

Boone slowed. They never talked about books. Mostly, Junie

liked to read the fantasy kind of stuff that Grace wrote. Ugh—
there she was again. He pushed the thought away.

"What is it?" he grumbled without looking at her.

"You know what."

Boone puzzled over this for a few seconds, until the impact
of her hint landed with a crash. He rounded on his cousin, who
didn't seem the least bit perturbed. "Will you just get over it?
Why do you care so much if I read that note, anyway?"

Junie lifted her chin. "Because Grace asked me to make sure
you got it. But I don't think you get it, Boone." She emphasized
the phrase *get it*.

"Just leave me alone about it, already. Please."

Junie's nostrils flared. "Fine. But just know that Grace put
that note into my hand herself. She *asked* me to give it to you. It
didn't magically appear. It wasn't some fake coincidence. It was
from *her*. The least you can do is read it." And she whirled
around and stormed back to her office, closing the door a little
too hard.

Whoa.

Boone wasn't sure he'd ever seen Junie get upset like this.
She was always fiery and overly passionate about things, but was
something else bothering her to make her continue pushing
Grace's note at him?

He made his way out through the snow to the barn where
Hazelnut waited. He rubbed a hand along her gray coat. "Ready
to head home, girl?"

Together, they made the stunning trek through the trees. In
spite of himself, Boone found he appreciated the sight of the
trees and landscape around him more than he had in a long
time. He had Grace to thank for that. Grace had found wonder
out here at every turn.

After getting Hazelnut situated in the barn, Boone went to
his cottage and started a fire. He reheated some pork chops and

green beans Aunt Meg had sent home with him the night before and sulked, drowning in his thoughts and Junie's taunts.

"She's right," he said to his fork. Junie had a point. The least he could do was read Grace's note.

The truth was, that note had haunted him every single day, and he was in some kind of bizarre war with himself, to prove how strong he was by resisting its temptation. It was like the equivalent of resisting the urge to violate customer privacy and look up Grace's information on the reservation she'd booked. Her phone number and address would be readily available to him from there.

He hadn't wanted to seem desperate. He'd ended things so thoroughly with her, there was little chance Grace would ever give him a second thought again.

Boone trekked into his bedroom and delved into his top drawer. He stared at Amy's necklace nestled beside the crumpled note. With shaking fingers, he pulled the note out and unfolded the paper's creases.

The words settled in with more impact than if she'd spoken them directly. He read them over and over. She wanted him. She wouldn't hate him if he showed up in Arizona tomorrow begging to see her again.

In that moment, he knew. Amy was unreachable for him now. Nothing could change the fact that she was gone. But Grace was still there. She'd said as much.

In a flash, Boone pulled open his phone. He didn't always get reception up here, and that was the case this time. "Stupid thing," he grumbled. What was the point of having a cell phone if he could never use it?

Boone considered revving up the snowmobile again, but the January snowfall had finally filled in all the gaping tracks he'd left behind the last time he'd been so foolhardy. Instead, he saddled Hazelnut and rode her back to the inn.

He left the horse with Troy in the barn and dashed into the house. It took all he had not to shout at Junie from the front the way he'd done when they were kids. Instead, he tipped his head toward the guests exploring the living room and turned toward Junie at the reception desk.

Junie jumped at his entrance. "Boone! What are you doing here? I thought you left."

He rested both of his hands on the counter. "Junie, can I borrow your mom's car?" He couldn't exactly take Hazelnut into town. There wasn't horse parking at the airport. He rolled his eyes at his own poor joke.

"Where are you going?" she asked.

"Better yet," he said, thinking it over, "I might need you to drop me off. Can you get someone to cover the desk for about an hour while you take me into town?"

He didn't have anything packed, but he always kept a bag here at the inn in the event of bad weather. He often stayed in his old room when snow kept him from heading back home. He could take that.

"What is going on? I can't just leave. You know we've been short on staff."

"I know," he said with regret. "I know, and I'll make it up to you. I'll make it all up to you." He should have helped her more. He shouldn't have been so grumpy and selfish. He had so much to make up to her for, and he fully intended to do just that. But he had to do something else first.

"Make what up to me? What happened? Are you okay?"

"The sleigh rides Christmas Eve. Not helping you here when you needed it. I'm sorry for shutting myself away for so long and I have you to thank for shaking me out of my rut."

Junie's eyes slitted. "Okay, who are you and what have you done with my cousin?"

He laughed, and it felt so good to release the sound.

Laughter came from everywhere inside of him. And then he bent at the waist, drew in the fullest breath he had in a good long while, and laughed some more. It was magic, pure and simple. So much around him was magic, so much he saw every day and yet never really *saw*.

He'd been so blind for far too long.

"Junie, I'm going to Arizona."

"You—you're what? Why?"

Boone grinned. Grinned! "I read her note, Junie. And I'm going to her."

"Boone—wait. You can't do that."

"Don't even think about stopping me. This is all your fault. Yours and that stupid radio's and Grace's too. I can't keep living the way I have been. I'm not a nice person anymore. I'm constantly grumpy—and those times you've called me out on it only made me grumpier because I knew you were right. I haven't been happy, Junie, but I haven't *allowed* myself to be happy. And I think it's time I did."

Junie blinked at him as if he were insane. Maybe he was, but he would fully accept the diagnosis. Then a smile spread over her lips as well. Redness blotched her cheeks the way it always did, and she laughed too. Soon, the two of them were standing there in the foyer of Harper's Inn. Laughing.

The guests in the living room stepped out. "Everything okay?" they asked.

"It's perfect!" Junie announced.

Boone pulled her into a hug. He felt lighter than he had in years. That would make the flight go by faster, for sure. He'd never been a fan of flying, but he'd do what he had to do if it meant trying to fix what he'd ruined with Grace.

Junie slapped his chest hard. "Now that you've come to your senses, my dear cousin, you can't run off to Arizona."

"I can't?"

"No," she said, straightening the collar of his wool-lined coat like a mother attempting to make her son look presentable. "Not without meeting our newest employee first."

He knew Junie relied on him a lot, but this was taking things a little far. "Did you hear what I said? You've been pushing me to go after Grace for weeks now. I tell you I'm doing that, and you want me to meet your newest employee first? I promise, I'll come back. I'm not abandoning you here."

"Will you stop talking?" Junie yanked his arm toward her office. Boone allowed it, willing but confused. She shoved him through the door and Boone nearly staggered.

Grace stood inside. Her long blonde hair swept down past her shoulders in curly waves the way it had the last time she was here. She wore a pink cardigan over a white shirt, and her blue eyes were wide with an emotion he couldn't name. Dread? Fear? Anticipation?

"Hi, Boone," she said. She gave him a timid, irresistible little smile.

Boone forgot all about Junie the instant he saw her. Her appearance had a physical reaction over him. His heart struck against his ribs like a bucking horse and he gasped from the effect.

He took a step forward. "You're the new employee?"

When? How? And why didn't Junie say anything to him before now? Actually, he was glad she didn't. He probably wouldn't have been ready to hear it.

Grace lifted a single shoulder. "I really missed this place back home. And then my mom gave me the idea, so I contacted Junie. She was all for an interview. We did it right there, on the phone. The next day I quit my job and...well, here I am."

"Here you are," he said stupidly. "But—why?"

"Why am I here?"

The strength was slowly draining from his body the longer

he stood apart from her. He took another step. Just one. "I mean, you missed the inn?"

A nod.

He couldn't believe how difficult it was to get the question out. "And—was the inn the only thing you missed?"

She licked her lips. He could practically feel the seconds skim over him as she slowly shook her head.

He took another step, feeling as though he was ready to burst with the effort of holding himself back. "I missed you too," he admitted.

The worry in her features melted. Her forehead relaxed, her cheeks pulling into a smile. This time she took a step. "I didn't want to leave in the first place," she said. "I left you a note."

"I got it."

"You did?" Her forehead puzzled. "And you read it?"

His last step closed the distance between them. His heart raced, and he lifted his hands to find hers. "Your words struck me right to the heart, Grace. I was just about to board a plane and come to *you*."

"Just about?" she asked, sounding confused. "When did you read it?"

"It may have taken me a few weeks to give in...."

She tinkled a laugh and he caught her in his arms as she pressed herself against him. Relief had never been so welcome. The embrace wove itself through him as if with invisible thread, sewing together his broken parts. He had many of them—so many. And they weren't all healed. But he could sense the beginning of it, behind his sternum and weaving its web through his ribs, keeping him together because she was in his arms. Because he was allowing her to be.

Grace buried her head into his shoulder. Boone held her, just held her, stroking his hands along her back, feeling the silk of her long hair, absorbing the beating of her heart. Her soft skin against his neck, the feel of her breathing moving her chest in time with his, he wanted to savor every sensation. He never wanted to let her go.

Her hand trailed up his spine, to the back of his neck, and her fingers brushed the shaved portion of his hair. It was like a spigot had turned, releasing all the stress and anger he'd been battling for weeks. Her touch allowed him to be himself, the man he'd been fighting for the last three years. She tilted her head and spoke against his throat. "I interviewed with Junie because I wanted you—well. I just wanted to be as close to you as I could."

He held her tighter at this admission. "Even though Christmas is over?"

She pulled away just enough to capture his gaze. Her eyes were a cerulean sea of blue, framed in by long lashes. She took a few moments to cast her gaze across his face, from his brow to his eyes to his mouth and back again. "Yes, and somehow, I'm as crazy for you now as I was back at your cottage."

She repositioned herself, standing back and lacing her fingers behind his neck. "Boone, the radio may have gotten us together, but I haven't heard any chimes in the air for a while, have you?"

He swallowed. His hands fisted at her waist. "No, I haven't."

"But I can't stop this otherworldly pull to be wherever you are. Magic got us to notice one another, but it isn't keeping us together. It's you."

"Me?"

"And me. It's us." She cast her gaze around the office before returning those crystal blue eyes to his. "The radio gave us a nudge, that's true, but the rest is up to us. I'm not ready to let you go." She inched closer again. Heat spilled from her body.

"No." It was a growl. He guided her the rest of the way, fully back in his arms where she belonged.

Grace released a little gasp, her eyes flicking to his. She licked her delectable mouth, took in his lips before saying, "I think we're just meant to be together and Santa knew it."

"Remind me to thank him sometime."

Boone was done talking. He wanted—needed—to let her know just how much she meant to him, just how much it meant to have her back at Harper's Inn, back in his embrace, and how this was the only place he wanted her to be. With him.

Her mouth was soft and accepting. It teased and captured while his hands couldn't hold enough of her. He pulled her tighter against him, gripping her hips, feeling her slim waist, enveloping her and keeping her as close as he could, and yet it wasn't anywhere near close enough.

"Thank him by letting Christmas into your heart, Boone," Grace said, flicking her long lashes open just enough to give him a glimpse of the sky in her eyes. "By letting me in."

He bent just enough for a lower hold on her. Wrapping his arms firmly around her, he lifted her so she rested her hands against his shoulders and peered down at him. "I'm letting you in and never letting go again," he said, gazing up at her. "You made my heart come back to life. I didn't know it could, and more still, I didn't think I could feel more for someone than I felt for Amy. We married young, but maybe love is like wine and gets better with age."

She cradled his face with her hands. "You just know more about life and it's harder to love when you've been wounded from it. That's probably why you're feeling more."

He lowered her to the ground. "I think *you're* why I'm feeling more. I'm sorry I ever let you go."

"How sorry?" she asked, nibbling her lip and eyeing his mouth once more.

"So sorry," he said with a breath, placing his mouth on hers.

EPILOGUE

Two years later

"What about this one?"

"Too scrawny."

Boone trudged a few paces away, bending backward as if trying to see just how high up the tree climbed. "This one?"

Grace shivered. She still wasn't good with being out in the snow for too long, though she loved to sit inside and stare out at its beauty often enough. Then again, she had Boone to warm her up whenever she got too cold.

She shook her head. "Too tall."

Her husband gave her an exasperated sigh. "You're impossible, woman," Boone said.

Grace cast her gaze across the forest landscape. Pine trees of every shape and size stood like spokes in the snow, spearing up toward the cloudless blue sky. Many of these would be too tall to fit in the little cottage they now shared.

"We need something with a little personality. Something short and squat."

Boone repositioned his grip on the chainsaw and glanced around. "Take your pick."

She trudged through the snow in new boots that were much better quality than from the first adventure she and Boone had taken in these woods. She also wore much thicker socks beneath the boots, so her toes were toasty warm. Her stomach grew queasier the longer she stood out in the cold, but they couldn't go back to the cottage without their tree. Boone had harnessed Hazelnut to a special kind of sled, one that would drag their Christmas tree behind the sleigh as they made their way back.

Everywhere she looked, the trees were just so...high. "I don't see anything short enough—wait." She rotated on the snow, gripping her stomach and waiting for the nausea to pass. She swallowed. There, behind her, stood the perfect little tree. Its branches weren't completely full, but it wasn't too high, and the scraggly branches bespoke of its character.

Boone crunched through the snow toward her. He wore his wool-lined coat, and a thick, fur hat that covered his ears. "This one? You're sure?"

"I'm sure." She took in the tree a final time, becoming emotionally attached to its stout stature. It was as if it was trying its hardest to be the kind of tree it was meant to be. She could already envision the colorful bulbs she intended to wreath it with.

"All right, then," he said. Taking a battle stance, he revved the chainsaw. It whirred to life, and he hacked into the trunk with mechanized power. Grace lost count, but soon enough, the little tree released a few cracking sounds and toppled to the snow.

She grinned with excitement and hurried back to where

Hazelnut stood with the sleigh. Gripping the horse's reins, she guided the mare to where Boone stood, inspecting the tree for any possible passengers.

Grace had already learned so much. Since she'd returned to Montana, she'd spent every possible hour in Boone's company. Junie hired her for upkeep and room checks. It was now Grace's job to clear the rooms once guests checked out, to replace bedding and look around for items that had been left behind. She also left little mints on the pillows and delivered fresh towels to each room. This saved Junie time enough to deal with balancing the books and the appointments.

Interestingly enough, Grace discovered another Christmas miracle. Usually the inn's rooms were booked for the Christmas season months and even years in advance. When Grace admitted one day that she'd managed to snag a room having booked it at the beginning of December of the same year she'd visited, it was nothing short of a wonder.

"Santa's radio," Boone and Junie had said in unison.

In any case, she'd also gotten much more accustomed to being around horses than she ever thought she would be. Boone had taught her how to clean, feed, saddle, and ride Hazelnut and the other horses around the inn. Junie joked that soon Grace would be driving the sleighs, but she declined. She was happy working inside, out of the cold.

Besides, soon enough she might be too busy to continue working at the inn anyway.

She had just received another rejection on her manuscript. She'd expected to snag a publishing contract right away because who wouldn't want her novel? She found she could handle the rejections a little easier this time around. Boone encouraged her in that regard—and he ended up being way better than any book boyfriend she'd ever read. He wasn't perfect, but then, neither was she. They had their fair share of squabbles, but they had a good time making up too.

Still, the books all over the shelves she'd had him build in their cottage were evidence that a girl still loved to read about a swoony hero once in a while.

"Ready to head back?" Boone asked.

"You bet." She climbed into the sleigh, trying to decide when and how to tell him the main reason she would be too busy to work much in the coming months. A romantic ride through the woods was the perfect setting for sharing secrets, after all. Still, she waited until they arrived back at their cottage.

Boone had wanted to marry here, but the inn was more accessible. This little place just didn't have the space to accommodate that many guests. Grace's parents had flown up from Arizona for the wedding, and Grace had worn a lovely, slim gown with simple white fabric and lace sleeves. And the bed she'd once shivered alone in now kept them both perfectly warm.

Grace braced open the cottage door and then ran out to help Boone with the tree. He was at its lower end, already lifting it by the trunk. She attempted to grip it around a few different places, but everywhere she tried branches ended up poking her in the face.

"Where am I supposed to hold it?"

Boone laughed and lowered his end. "Here, switch me places."

Grace did so. The trunk end was much easier to grip. Boone carried most of the weight, she could tell, but she did her best to keep up and help get the little tree into their house.

Soon enough, it was positioned in the stand they'd prepped beforehand, in place of where the dining table usually sat by the window. Grace poured water into the base, breathing in deep and relishing the natural pine scent.

"Mmm, that is so delicious," she said, standing. Boone was ready with a strand of lights and together, they trimmed the tree. The old curtains in the cottage had been replaced by rustic, modern prints. Grace had insisted they take down anything that wasn't directly Boone's—which was a lot—and begin to fill the walls with their own memories. Not that she had anything against his family or heritage, but this was their home. She didn't want to spend her hours here looking at things that had no emotional connection to her.

Boone had built her a bookshelf, and it stood in the empty space near the door leading to their bedroom and bathroom. They both filled it with even more books, and someday, Grace hoped it would hold some written by her as well.

Junie joked around about them taking the radio to their house, but Boone and Grace both declined. "We've had enough help from that thing, thank you very much," Boone had said.

"What do you think happened to that couple, Lacie and Jared? The ones who claimed to be married by a snowman. Do you think they stayed married?" Grace had asked after they'd made their trek back home that night. The trek home was almost her favorite part of the day. Sometimes they rode horses, sometimes they rode in the sleigh. In the summertime the forest was filled with bird calls and creaking twigs as they went. No matter what time of year, that walk with him was the highlight of the day. It meant work was done, and they had nothing else to do but be together.

"I'm not sure," Boone said. "I don't exactly keep tabs on the guests who come and go."

"Wouldn't it be fun to know how else the radio messed with people's lives? Who else could it have tampered with?"

"Junie and Mason for one," Boone said.

"Yeah, but she's never really told us what happened. Besides, they aren't even together now. I'd love to tap into Lacie and Jared's story and see how things went."

"I guess we'll never know," Boone said.

"There is one more story, though," Grace said. "I have the best Christmas present for you."

"Oh? Why not wait until Christmas to tell me?"

"Because I think you're going to start wondering why I'm not feeling all that great right now."

Boone's gaze flicked down her body and back to her face again. "You're not?"

Grace placed a hand on her stomach. "No. I'm feeling sick. Your aunt loaned me this book about it. They tell me the nausea will last the first few months..."

Boone's brows leapt to his hairline. "Grace, are you trying to tell me you're expecting?"

She grinned, loving the delight dawning on his face. "We won't be able to wrap his or her presents since whoever this baby is won't be born until July, but—"

She didn't get to finish. Boone gathered her in his arms and spun in a circle. "My Grace. I love you so much. I always felt like letting myself love again, start a family again, would be betraying Amy and our baby. But I'm so glad it's not."

She leaned into him, breathing him in. "What made you change your mind?"

"You," he said. "And Junie. And a crazy, magical radio. It's okay for us to be happy, Grace. To find joy in our lives. You were right; Amy would have wanted this for me, because I would have wanted it for her."

Grace rested her head against his chest. "If it's a girl, I want to name her Amy, Boone."

His hand stroked her stomach. "Are you sure?"

"In honor of your wife."

"How about Amy Grace?"

Grace smiled at that. "And if it's a boy?"

He quirked a brow mischievously. "What about Santa?"

Her brows snapped down. "You're kidding, right?"

"Nicholas, then. He did bring us together, after all."

She would give him that much. "Hmm. Good point. You can't tell me you would have given me the time of day otherwise."

Boone laughed and dipped his face into the space between her head and her shoulder. "You're right, though that doesn't mean I didn't notice the beautiful blonde woman who barged her way into my conversation with a little girl."

"Darn right. I had to get you to talk to me."

"I'm glad you did."

Her heart thundered in her chest. There was no rejection in this, not anymore. Not ever again. She had never been happier in her entire life than she'd been married to Boone Harper. And Grace couldn't wait to see what their child would look like. She hoped the baby had his chocolate brown eyes.

What was it Grace had thought about fictional men being better than men in real life? Boone surpassed every man in every way. She couldn't believe she'd found someone who fit her so perfectly.

Or maybe, she could believe. All thanks to a meddlesome, antique radio.

"I love you," she said. "Merry Christmas, Boone."

His hands wrapped around her waist. "Merry Christmas," he said. "I love you too."

∼

Thanks for reading! More Santa's radio romances are coming, including Junie and Mason's story and Lacie and Jared's. Join Catelyn Meadows' newsletter to stay updated at www.catelynmeadows.com!

~

Read the next Snowed in for Christmas clean holiday romance, Snowed In at the Ranch!

Copyright © 2020 Cortney Pearson
All rights reserved.
No part of this publication may be reproduced, stored in or
introduced into a retrieval system or transmitted, in any form or
by any means—electronic, mechanical, printing, recording, or
otherwise—without the prior permission of the author, except
for use of brief quotations in a book review.

This book is a work of fiction. Names, characters, organizations,
places, incidents, or events are either products of the author's
imagination or are used fictitiously. Any resemblance to actual
events, locales or persons, living or dead, is entirely coincidental.

Beta Read by Naomi Naihi
Cover Design by Steve Novak
Author Photo by Clayton Photo + Design

www.catelynmeadows.com

Made in the USA
Coppell, TX
15 November 2023

24300088R00125